seven
PAPER
SKIES

USA TODAY BESTSELLING AUTHOR
YOLANDA OLSON

Cover and Formatting by Pretty in Ink Creations

Editing by Insta-Love Author Services

We were supposed to be best friends forever, but
life has a way of throwing curveballs at you.

The time we spent together was something I knew
that I would cherish forever.

Forever.

A word I thought meant a lifetime as a child,
though now I know it means something different.

I was glad to find him again so we could have one
more lifetime together.

I kept my secret as long as I could because I
wanted him to remember me as I was, not as what
I had become.

Best friends forever or until the road ends?

Prologue

DOUGIE

I was standing in the doorway to the bedroom, staring at the ugly black and white circular wallpaper. My arms were crossed over my chest, and I leaned against the doorframe with a heavy sigh. I had been meaning to rip down that hideous design for a while, but Jellyfish loved it so much that I didn't have the heart to do it. I didn't even have the courage or will to walk into that room after she left me.

There were days where I would stand in the doorway, like today, and try to catch a small breath of her lingering scent. Jelly always smelled faintly of papyrus on a cool, sunny day, and even though she had been gone for quite a while, I could almost swear there were days that I could faintly smell her.

I closed my eyes and tried to hear her laughter again. It was so high pitched and full of genuine happiness that it would make anyone that could hear her at least smile or laugh along.

Jelly was very free spirited. She was so small, short and petite, with the biggest fire for adventure inside of her. She always wore a peasant dress of some sort, with cherry-red boots (always red boots, regardless of the color of the dress) and would wear her long, wavy brown hair loose. It would be always adorned with a flower hairband of some sort. Her big blue eyes were always full of happiness and mischief and drew me in from the first time I saw her when I was a young boy of six years old.

I opened my eyes and glanced at the dresser that held her hairbands and smiled. Jelly got her nickname because of the Flower Hat Jellyfish; one of her favorite animals and why she wore the flower pieces. She always said that she wanted to be as free as a jellyfish and just as beautiful. And no matter how many times you told her that she already was, she'd never believe it.

With one last sigh, I flipped off the light switch in the room and closed the door behind me as I backed out of the doorway.

I walked through the small, sunny kitchen and into the living room where I dropped down onto the shaggy maroon rug. On the small wooden table to my left was a book of pictures we had made of all of our adventures, and I reached for it. Leaning back against the ragged couch behind me, I crossed my legs underneath myself and opened the book.

I went straight to the last picture first and snapped it shut almost immediately. It was the last picture Jelly and I had taken together, and it cut like a knife still to see it.

I took a deep, shaky breath and blinked back tears as I opened the book again, careful to start on the very first page.

I smiled sadly. It was a picture of me at six and Jelly at five, around the time we had first met. We were standing in my parents' living room, and she was in one of her peasant dresses and cherry-red boots with her fingers inside of her mouth, pulling the sides widely and sticking out her tongue. Her brown hair was in pigtails, and she had managed to weave small flowers into them.

As for me, always the taller of the two, I had an arm on top of her head and was giving the camera a thumbs up with a huge smile in my fashionable dark blue suspender pants and mustard-brown sweater. I chuckled at myself, looking at the big head of long, curly black hair I used to have, and the flower she had managed to somehow tangle into it.

I pulled out the picture carefully and read the back.

Jellyfish and Toady
Five and Six - 1962.

My older brother nicknamed me Toad because he said I had a habit of following Jelly's every lead on everything she wanted to do.

I couldn't help it, though. She was my very best and only friend when I was a kid. Well, not only friend, but the one I spent the most time with.

I put the picture back in its place and flipped the page. The next few were of our birthdays; seventh and eighth, respectively.

The pictures of Jelly on her seventh birthday were as follows.

The first was of me handing her a poorly handmade flower hairband and her small hands on either side of her face in shock. The second was of her pulling me into a hug, and me trying to look grossed out. Because, you know, girls equal cooties when you're that young. The third and last picture I had from that day was of her happily wearing the flower hairband, which had already fallen apart on top of her head, and smiling widely. I had my arm around her shoulders, and she had her arms wrapped around me as we both smiled at the camera.

The pictures of my eighth birthday went a little something like this.

Jelly and I out in my parents' backyard, covered in mud because of the rainstorm we refused to run from. The second was of us inside with towels wrapped around our shoulders, dirt caked on our faces, and smiling like we had just committed some great act of nonconformity. The next one was of her sitting next to me on the floor while I opened my presents, and the last one was of her kissing me on the cheek after I had opened the small package of green army soldiers she had saved up to buy me.

I still had most of them hidden away in a little box for safekeeping. The first gift Jelly ever gave me; my most prized possessions.

I sighed and flipped through a few more pages until I came across her tenth birthday. She was hugging something closely to her chest; so closely, in fact, that if you weren't there, you wouldn't have known what it was.

One day after school, we walked past one of the local toy stores and saw a doll that caught her attention in ways I had never seen before. It was small, kind of rag-dollish and mostly red. I remembered her putting her hands on the window and whispering into the glass about how it was the most beautiful thing she had ever seen.

That day, after we got home from school, I ran to my room and pulled out an old coffee tin from its hiding place underneath my bed. I kept all of my change and allowance money in it and had been saving to buy a new bike that I really wanted.

I spilled out the contents onto the floor and believed that I had counted twelve dollars and thirty six cents before I dropped it all back in.

I smiled thinking of how quickly I ran back to the toy store, terrified that it had been sold in the hour I had been home.

I felt excited when I saw that it was still sitting in the window, and I ran in with my coffee tin full of money and went straight to the window display. After I fished it out, I went to stand in line with what I was sure would be the best present she would receive for her birthday.

When it was my turn, I carefully placed the doll on the counter and spilled out my coffee tin. I wasn't sure how much the doll cost, but I was sure I had enough.

"Seven dollars and sixty cents," the friendly old man behind the counter had told me.

I looked at the doll for a moment, visions of my new bike flying out of my head, before I shrugged and counted out the amount.

You have to understand that in 1966, seven dollars was *a lot* of money. But if she loved it, I would've spent every dime I had on it.

7

And she did. She cried when she pulled it from the shoddy wrapping paper I had wrapped it with and hugged it to her chest so tightly, I was waiting for the stuffing to fly out.

The next year, her family moved away from Baker City, Oregon to an undisclosed location.

It would be another seven years before I saw her again.

I closed the picture album and placed it on the table again. I looked around our apartment one last time before I walked out into the beautiful spring day, wondering if I'd ever see her again.

One

JELLYFISH

September 1973

"Class, can I have your attention? We have a new student transferring in for her last year. Please say hello to Miss —"

"Jelly's fine," I interceded, with the wave of a hand.

I glanced around the room and smiled at everyone in turn. I was damn lucky I had been able to get into this school without any transcripts, but I missed home. So much that I hitchhiked my way from Marfa, Texas all the way back just in time for school to start.

"Miss, we go by our real names in this class," Mr. Whatever said to me seriously.

"Far out. Mine is Jellyfish, but you can call me Jelly," I replied with a wink as I walked toward an empty desk at the back and sat down.

I glanced to the girl on my right who was grinning ear to ear. I grinned back and slid my bag under my desk before I turned to look at the boy to my left.

He was staring at me intensely, and his knuckles were white from how hard he was griping the front of his desk. I raised an eyebrow at him, and his face turned beet red before he looked away.

I turned back to the girl on my right and leaned over.

"What's his problem?" I asked in a whisper, jerking my head in the boy's direction.

She glanced past me and grinned before leaning toward me.

"That's Dougie. He's a lot of fun. Real ladies' man, if you know what I mean," she whispered before the teacher smacked his desk for our attention.

We separated angelically and passed notes for the rest of the class. I found out her name was Beverly Thomas. I told her that she could call me

Jelly or Jellyfish. I wasn't too keen on people knowing my real name.

When the class let out forty minutes later, I told her I would meet her in the cafeteria for lunch. I wanted to stop by my locker and put away my books first.

We parted ways before we got to the door and, I was greeted by Dougie who had been waiting just outside.

"Hey," he said quietly.

"Dougie the Ladies' Man!" I exclaimed with a grin. "How are you?"

"You can't believe everything that Bev tells you," he replied, rolling his eyes.

"Walk me to my locker," I said with a laugh.

He nodded and fell into step beside me, but he was so quiet and seemed so nervous that *I* was starting to get nervous, too.

"So are you from here?" he asked, when we reached my locker. I fidgeted with the combination a few times before I finally got it open.

"Originally, yeah. I've lived in Marfa for about seven years though. What a drag," I replied, shaking my head.

"Marfa? " he asked curiously.

"Texas."

"Oh."

I put my books away and spun the lock after I had secured it back in place. I turned to face Dougie who was still looking ungodly nervous.

"Are you okay?"

He bit his lip and looked down for a moment, rubbing the back of his neck uneasily. He looked like he really wanted to say something but was almost too terrified.

"I'm not going to bite you. I'm all about peace and love," I assured him, giving his arm a pat.

"And the flower hairbands. And the peasant dresses. And the red boots. Still. After all these years," he said softly.

"I always have been," I said with a laugh.

"Yeah, I know," he said looking into my eyes for the first time.

I took a nervous step back. Something in the way he said that made me feel very uncomfortable all of a sudden. Though I couldn't shake that he seemed familiar for some reason with those black, soft curls; his chestnut brown eyes. He really did remind me of someone.

"So listen, Bev's waiting for me. I don't want to be rude on the first day of school, you know? Maybe we'll have another class together," I said, taking small steps backwards.

He looked at me and held my gaze for a moment before he nodded. As I turned and walked away, I could feel his eyes burning into me, but I didn't turn around.

I made my way into the cafeteria and waved at Beverly when I saw her. Then I walked over to the lunch line and picked up a tray, hoping that charm would be able to pay for the food since I didn't have any money.

I was starving. It had been a solid two days in a car with no stops to get back to Baker City in time for me to start school. I was piling all kinds of treats onto my tray. Cookies, pudding, and fruit cups before I finally grabbed two sandwiches and a soda pop.

The cashier was eyeing my tray when I reached her as she started to punch the numbers into the register. My hands were shaking so hard that I had to put the tray down. I still wasn't sure what I was going to do when she asked for the money. Probably just grab the tray and run as fast as I could.

Hunger was bogus, and I was dying to feed the beast inside.

"That'll be three dollars and fifty seven cents," the lady said to me.

I smiled sweetly and began to pat the sides of my dress, knowing full well that I didn't have any pockets. I actually spent a solid minute doing that before she blew out her breath impatiently.

"If you don't have any money, then you can't have the food," she said loudly.

I felt myself flush with embarrassment as a couple of kids at nearby tables snickered. I sighed heavily and hungrily as I pushed the tray toward her. I started to walk away from the line when I felt a hand on my arm.

"I told you to wait for me."

I turned slightly around and saw Dougie the Ladies' Man with his own tray. He gave me a small smile before he told the lady to ring us up together.

He handed my tray back to me after he paid for our lunches. I looked up at him for a moment, and he just stared back at me.

"Thanks, man," I said quietly.

Dougie nodded, held my gaze again for a moment longer, and walked off to join his friends. I made my way toward Bev's table and sat down. She introduced me to her friends, but I was so busy stealing glances at Dougie that I missed most of their names. The far out thing was that Doug was looking at me, too. I decided on the next glance I would smile and see what he would do.

"Jellyfish?" Bev asked, laughing and nudging me.

The girl that was sitting across from me followed my gaze. She saw that I had been staring at Doug and turned back with a huge grin.

"He's a major hunk, isn't he?"

I shrugged and took a bite of my sandwich. The beast inside of me growled hungrily, so I took another bite, and another, until the sandwich was gone.

"He doesn't have a girlfriend, you know. Not last that I heard, anyway. I can always get the skinny if you want me to," she said, still grinning.

"That's groovy. I'm not really interested," I replied, grabbing my pudding.

The girl (Beverly reintroduced her as Peggy) and Bev exchanged a knowing glance. I rolled my eyes and reached for my plastic spoon. While they started talking again, I took the opportunity to glance at Doug's table again and saw that he was already looking in my direction.

I smiled widely, and he chuckled. Then he smiled back, and I felt myself blush. I put a huge scoop of pudding into my mouth and turned my attention back to the girls.

Maybe life could actually be normal again. A few girlfriends to hang out with should help.

Maybe Baker City was the safest place for me to be. After all, it was my real home, even though I didn't have anywhere to live yet.

Maybe I have a huge crush, I thought, scoping out Doug again.

Two

The final bell rang, signaling the end of the school day as I was heading toward my locker. I set my bag down on the floor as I started to fidget with the combination. After about three tries I got it open and told myself to steal a padlock sometime soon.

I pulled open the locker door and reached for my bag to start loading the school books in when an envelope caught my eye. My curiosity piqued in full force, and I grabbed it. Turning it over, I saw that someone had crudely drawn a jellyfish and a frog on the front, and my hands started to shake slightly.

Sliding a long fingernail underneath the flap, I ripped it carefully open and pulled out an old picture. A picture that I hadn't seen in a very long time with a friend that I hadn't forgotten in the time that I was gone. A friend that I loved and missed more than I could ever put into words.

I looked around the hallway, desperately hoping that I might see who left this for me. Someone knew who I was, and even though it worried me, they might be able to tell me where Toad was, too.

"Hey Jellyfish! What are you looking at?"

I turned to my left and saw Bev and Peggy approaching me with friendly smiles. Both of which faded, of course, when they saw my tear stained face.

They rushed the rest of the way toward me, and Beverly gently pried the picture out of my hand. She examined it for a moment with a smile.

"Is this you?" she asked. I nodded and blinked back tears.

Peggy leaned over Bev's arm to take a better look at the photo and she looked up at me with raised eyebrows.

"Is that ... *Doug?*" she asked in shock.

"What?" I asked, snatching the picture back. I stared at the little boy next to me, with his arm on top of my head grinning like a champion. Then I thought of the young man who watched me with such intensity when I first got to class, paid for my lunch when I was so hungry, and shared stolen glances with me.

Oh, my God. It is *Toad!*

I took off running down the length of the hallway, pushing open every classroom door that I could. Now that I knew, I had to find him. The world would finally make sense again if I had Toady with me.

Beverly and Peggy were running behind me, trying to get me to stop. They were yelling something about me going the wrong way.

"Stop!" Peggy said, grabbing hold of my arm and pulling me to a halt. "Dougie is always outside after school. If you go toward the football field, you'll see a grassy knoll. That's where he hangs out with his friends before he goes home."

"Which way?" I asked breathlessly.

"Come on," Bev said, taking me by the hand. The three of us ran back the way we came and out the double doors in the back of the school. We ran toward the football field, and when I saw the knoll that Peggy was talking about, I ripped free from them and ran faster than ever.

I saw him. He was standing up and talking to a group of guys about our age. They were all laughing about something, and at the angle Dougie was standing, he never saw me coming.

When I reached him, I threw myself as hard as I could at him, knocking him down to the ground and landing on top of him sideways.

"Whoa!" he yelled as we lay there crumpled on the grass. He turned his face to look at me, and I gave him the biggest, happiest smile in the world. Dougie started laughing and rolled onto his back, crossing his arms behind his head.

"Ever think of joining the football team?" he asked with a grin.

I laughed and put my head on his chest. I closed my eyes and inhaled deeply, forgetting that we weren't alone, but also not caring at what anyone else was thinking.

"That was fast, Doug," one of his friends joked.

I opened my eyes again and got to my feet. I leaned down and pulled Dougie to his feet, and we stood there for a second just grinning at each other like fools.

"Actually, it took long enough," he said to him, still looking at me.

"Sorry! It's been seven years! How was I supposed to know?" I asked, throwing my hands up.

"I knew it the moment you said 'Jellyfish'," he replied with mock hurt on his face.

"Good Lord, Jellyfish! You sure can boogie!" Bev said when she and Peggy finally reached us.

"What exactly is going on here?" another one of Dougie's friends asked. I finally tore my gaze away from him and held up the picture so that they could see it.

They all started to laugh good-naturedly at the picture of two young, best friends. I crossed my arms loosely over my chest as they passed it around and glanced back at Doug.

"I can't believe you still have that."

"Oh, I have lots of stuff," he replied with a mischievous grin.

"Like what?" I asked curiously.

"I guess you'll have to come over to find out."

"I think we all should," Bev interceded with a laugh.

21

"Gnarly! Let's go!" one of his friends shouted as the group started to walk toward the parking lots.

I grabbed Doug by the arm and held up a hand. I waited until the others were out of earshot before I turned him to face me. I held his hands in mine and I looked up into his curious eyes and I smiled.

"I love you, Douglas Kenison."

He smiled. "I love you, too –"

"Tut, tut! I will have none of that," I replied, stopping him from calling me by my given name.

He took my hand in his and laughed, "I was going to say, 'I love you, too, Jellyfish,' but you stopped me."

"Oh. Sorry," I said, making a face.

He grinned and pulled me into a tight hug. He took a deep breath and let it out into my hair. I looked off into the distance, wondering if I could remember the last time I was this happy.

But it also made me wonder.

"To be clear, we're talking about platonic love right? Not mushy love," I said into his chest.

"Right."

"Good."

There was nothing I could do about the crush that I had developed so quickly. But I could probably just attribute it to my heart knowing who he really was even though my head didn't. Yeah, that had to be it.

"God, I've missed you," he said softly, hugging me tighter.

I sighed deeply.

"What's on your mind, little mama?" he asked.

"I just can't believe it," I replied, shaking my head.

"What?"

"That you're there and I'm here. It's almost like I left a nightmare and walked into a dream," I said. "You have no idea how much I've honestly missed you."

"Yes, I do. Jelly, I was crushed when you left and I have been for years. You were my best friend, and we spent every day together. Then one morning, you didn't come out of your house to go to school, and I sat there. For the entire day, I just sat there. I don't know what I was really waiting for because something told me you were gone. But I

23

didn't want to leave in case you happened to come back. I didn't want to miss it, you know?"

"I know," I replied softly, looking away.

I took a deep breath, thinking of the moment that I needed him most and he wasn't there. It wasn't his fault because he didn't know where I was. And it wasn't my fault; I kept telling myself that so I could find a way to live with what happened.

We finally pulled apart, and Dougie told me that he would walk me to my home. He said that I could come over tomorrow when there wasn't a crowd and we could catch up on the seven years that we had missed. That's when I decided I should be partially honest with him. I'd be wholly honest once I was sure I could trust him again.

"You know that bag you insisted on carrying?" I asked, gesturing toward it. Peggy had been smart enough to grab it when I went on my hunt for Dougie.

"Yeah."

"Everything I own in this world is in that bag. I actually just got into town last night so I don't have a place to stay yet."

24

"Where are your parents?" he asked curiously.

I felt myself become a little woozy at the question. I was afraid he would ask me that. But instead of answering, I took my bag from him.

"So it's not necessary for you to walk me home because I haven't figured out where I'm staying yet," I explained lightly. "I'll see you in school tomorrow!"

I gave Doug a wave and started to walk away when his serious tone of voice stopped me. That and the fact that he wound up using my full and real name.

"Are you in some kind of trouble?" he asked, giving me a lingering stare.

"Me? In trouble? No way!" I replied with an uneasy laugh.

He eyed me for a moment before he took the bag from me and slung it over his shoulder again. I reached for the bag and he gently smacked my hand away. I looked at him suspiciously, but when he took my hand and kissed it, I just smiled shyly.

"Let's go home. I'm sure Mom and Dad will be surprised to see you. Though, I don't know how

I'm going to convince them to let you stay with us," he said, putting an arm around my shoulders. "Not to mention, I'm sure everyone is wondering where we are."

"You don't think they'll try to call my parents, do you?" I asked nervously as we walked down the block.

"They can't. They don't know that they're in Marfa, and something tells me you won't give up their phone number anyway," he replied dryly.

Good point.

We walked in silence the rest of the four blocks until we reached our destination. I smiled and pulled away from him as I rested my hands on the gates.

It was like going back in time to the happiest days of my life before the nightmare took over and turned my world upside down. I looked down at the flowers that his mother apparently kept replanting year after year and smiled. They were the same flowers that my Toady had ripped up to make my hairband when we were kids.

"Doug? Your other friends are already inside. And who's that you've got with you? "

I turned my attention back toward the front door of the house and smiled widely.

"Well, you just don't age, do you Mrs. K?" I asked, putting my hands on my hips.

"Thank you?" she asked looking slightly confused. She looked at Doug then back at me a bit wearily. Almost as if she didn't know what to do.

"Mom: flowers, dress, red boots? Can't you tell that it's Jellyfish?" he finally asked, laughing.

She inhaled sharply and her hands flew to her mouth. Once it settled in, she ran off of the front steps and pulled me into a hug almost as tight as I had given him.

"Oh, sweetheart! It's been so long! I'm sorry I didn't recognize you," she said, pulling back and brushing my hair behind my ears. I felt my face turn red, and I just stood there with a goofy grin as she stepped back to take me in. "You've grown so much!"

"Not height wise," Doug said matter-of-factly.

I turned around and playfully smacked him on the arm, causing him and his mother laugh.

"Where are your parents, Jellyfish?" she asked me. "I'd love to see them again!"

I cut my eyes nervously toward Dougie, and he sprang into action.

"So yeah, we're just gonna head into the basement. Is that where everyone else is?" he asked her, pulling me along behind him.

"Yes, of course! My manners are so terrible these days," she said apologetically. "I'll bring some snacks down for everyone in a little while. Have fun kids!"

Dougie dropped my bag by the door and led me down into the spacious basement area. He explained that this was where his family entertained guests.

"I'll see if I can talk them into letting you stay down here for a while," he said quietly as we joined the others.

"Thanks," I replied, squeezing his hand.

The seven of us spent the next two hours going through old photos. I smiled at how neatly and carefully he kept them in small photo albums. One of the books was dedicated completely to our childhood while the others were a mixture of his family, my family, and him and me.

When everyone left and I lingered behind, his parents looked at each other a little worriedly and asked me to stay for dinner.

And that's where things got really interesting.

Three

This is how the uncomfortable dinner conversation went.

Mrs. K: It really is so nice to see you again, Jellyfish. Is your family in town just visiting or are you moving back to Baker City?

Me: (mumbling) Um. I'm finishing my last semester of high school here. My parents didn't come.

Mr. K: Oh? Where are they?

Me: Home.

Mrs. K: Where is it exactly that you moved away to, anyway?

(I shot a desperate glance at Dougie who once again saved the day.)

Doug: I thought that we couldn't talk at dinner?

Mrs. K: (confused) We never said that.

Doug: (meaningfully) Oh, that's right! It was not to talk with our mouths full. You should have some bread, *Mom.*

Mr. K: Douglas, watch your tone with your mother please.

(Doug grunts. I put a fork of homemade garlic mashed potatoes in my mouth and pray for the questions to stop. No such luck.)

Mrs. K: So, your parents let you travel alone? Where did you say they were?

Doug: Mom. Bread. Have some.

Mr. K: Douglas, I'm going to tell you *one more time* and that's it.

(Dougie sighs heavily and drops his fork. It clatters loudly on the plate and he turns to look at me.)

Doug: So, tell me all about your life. Where have you been? Where are you hiding your parents? Why did you leave them behind? Did you kill them? You killed them, didn't you? Did you hide the bodies in a good place? Who else have you killed while you were away? Has your spree stopped? Trip on any drugs? What kind? Do you have any on you? Can I have some?

(And he rambled on. I didn't understand what exactly he was doing so all I do is nod or shake my head correspondingly to the questions as they fly out. Finally, Mr. K. yelled at him.)

Mr. K: Douglas, go to your room and stay there. But first, walk your friend out, then come back and apologize to your mother.

Doug: Actually, I was hoping that you'd let little Jellyfish stay with us for a while.

Me: No, it's okay.

(I get to my feet and push my chair in. I'm on my way to the front door when Dougie catches up to me and grabs my bag. I reach for it, but he heads back down into the basement and disappears for a few moments. I'm standing there with my arms wrapped nervously around myself when he finally reappears.)

Doug: Come on. I set up the room, and you can stay downstairs.

Mrs. K: (entering the living room) Excuse me! We didn't agree on that.

Doug: *Mom. It's Jellyfish, not a stranger.* If anyone should be allowed to stay with us, it's her.

Mr. K: I have no problem with this as long as you let your parents know that you're safe. And you (he points at Dougie) stay out of the basement while she's down there.

(Dougie rolls his eyes, and we go into the kitchen. He picks me up and sets me on the counter and hands me the phone. I must have looked like a deer caught in headlights because he winked and dialed the number zero ten times. He motioned for me to fake talk as quickly as I could and then hang up the phone.)

Me: All set. Thanks Mr. and Mrs. K. They said to tell you hello and to thank you for letting me stay for a little bit.

They looked at each other for a moment before nodding. Mr. K looked at the stairs that led to the second floor and gave Doug a meaningful look. Mrs. K, I noticed, was eyeing me a little oddly now but eventually walked back into the kitchen. Probably to clean up. Mr. K stared at the both of us for a moment before he left us standing there and went upstairs. I turned to face Dougie who was sitting on the arm of the couch smiling at me. He held out his hand, and I took it, letting him lead me down the stairs into the basement.

Four

"They can be so weird sometimes," he remarked once we got comfortable. He was lying back in a dark brown recliner while I sat down on a psychedelic blue and black rug.

"I don't know. I think they were asking legit questions," I replied with a shrug.

Dougie glanced at me over the side of the chair. It wasn't because I looked at him that I knew, it was because I felt his eyes on me again. It was the intense stare he gave me in the classroom. It was the intense stare he gave me while watching me practically run down the hallway at school.

"What?" I finally asked, glancing up at him.

"You're really, really pretty," he said finally. "I'd say foxy, but I want to be sincere about it. Because you are, Jelly; you're *really* pretty."

I felt myself turn as red as my boots, which I now found myself staring at. I wanted to tell Dougie how handsome he turned out, because he really did. I had never expected little Toad to turn into hunky Doug. But my last experience with a hunk went horribly wrong, so I kept it to myself.

"Thanks," I replied softly.

He smiled and turned his attention back to the television, which I found odd because it wasn't even on. Sighing, I scooted closer to his recliner and rested my head against it. I wanted to tell Dougie about the reason I ran away from Marfa. I knew that if anyone understood, it would be him. But I wasn't sure if he would still love me when he knew what happened, and I didn't want to take that chance.

"What happened to you in Marfa?" he suddenly asked quietly.

"Huh?"

"You came back different. I was able to tell when you walked into the classroom. I've been wanting to ask you all day but we haven't had a chance to be alone until now."

I pulled my legs up to my chest and shook my head. Dougie got out of the recliner and sat down on the rug next to me. An involuntary shudder ran through me when he put an arm around my shoulders, but the gesture calmed me. It made me feel *safe*.

"I don't want to talk about it," I replied.

"Will you tell me one day?" he asked, resting his cheek on top of my head.

I nodded.

We heard a set of footsteps descending into the basement and Doug sighed. It was either his mother or father, neither of which would be happy he was down here with an arm around me.

I put my hand on his and tried to pry his arm away, but he wouldn't budge. Instead he just looked at me with the mischievous Toad grin I used to see as a child, and I couldn't help but giggle.

"Douglas! We told you that you couldn't be down here with Jellyfish. Please go to your room," Mrs. K scolded as she peeked her head into the room.

"Mom, can I talk to you for a second? Upstairs? In private?" he asked, getting to his feet.

She looked at the both of us suspiciously before nodding. Dougie kissed me on top of the head and got to his feet.

"I'll be right back," he whispered. I looked up at him and nodded and watched his mother follow him up the stairs.

I hugged my legs tighter and closed my eyes. I put my forehead against my knees and thought of that night in Marfa. The all-night rave that led to the drugs was my first experience—with raves and drugs. It was also my last. I had taken a bad hit of acid and—

"Jellyfish, can you come up here?" Mrs. K called from upstairs.

I shook the memory away and took a deep, steadying breath before I got to my feet. I stood in place for about thirty seconds, breathing deeply and forcing a fake smile onto my face, and then climbed the stairs.

Mrs. K was standing with her arms folded over her chest just outside the door, and Dougie was leaning against the kitchen counter. He smiled when he saw me, and I smiled back. When I looked at Mrs. K again and saw how serious she looked, my smile disappeared.

"Yes?" I asked timidly.

"Doug tells me that you had some trouble in Marfa. You won't tell him what it is, which leads me to wonder why you're here. I have to ask you some questions, Jellyfish. Did you run away?" she asked.

"Yes."

She sighed heavily, but continued, "Did it have to do with your parents."

"No," I whispered, a tear rolling down my cheek. Doug reached forward and took my hand. I glanced at him and smiled weakly.

"Are you in trouble with the law?" she asked quietly.

"No."

"Do your parents know where you are?"

"Obviously not if she ran away, Mom," Doug said, pulling me into a hug.

Mrs. K looked at him sharply before turning her attention back to me.

"Are you in trouble of any kind?"

I shook my head. The truth was I didn't know. I hadn't been feeling too good lately, and I knew I needed to go to the doctor again, but I kept putting off.

"Will you tell us what happened?"

I looked at her, holding her gaze before I answered. "I'll tell Dougie. *Only* Dougie, but I won't tell him anytime soon. I appreciate you letting me stay here Mrs. K, but I don't trust anyone but Toad anymore."

She took a deep breath and let it out in a long sigh. I was feeling nervous; almost as if she were going to tell me that I couldn't stay there now because I wouldn't tell her about that night in Marfa.

Instead, much to my shock, she told Dougie that he could stay with me in the basement for the first few nights until I felt "normal" again. She made us both swear that nothing inappropriate would happen, and if it did, I would have to leave immediately, and she would notify my parents of my whereabouts.

Then I'll have to run again, I thought miserably. There was no way I'd go back to Texas; wild horses wouldn't be able to drag me back.

But, nonetheless, we agreed, and Doug hugged his mother in thanks. She nodded and looked at me kindly before hugging me as well and heading upstairs.

"Inappropriate?" Dougie asked as I followed him down the stairs. "I don't think anything we would do could be considered inappropriate. Do you?"

I didn't answer. I just kept my head down and took my spot on the rug again. I thought of what his mother said and about feeling normal. It would never happen. Not even in a thousand lifetimes would I feel like I would ever be normal again. Hell, I didn't even know what normal was anymore, much less how to get back to it.

I watched Dougie as he took some small pillows off of the ragged couch that was on the other side of his recliner. When he began to unfold it, I realized that it was bed, too.

"I usually sleep on the right. I hope that's okay with you," he said, picking up the pillows and placing them back onto the bed.

"You're … sleeping down here? With me?" I asked in semi-shock.

"Well, yeah. I mean, unless you consider that inappropriate," he replied with a grin. "I know *they* sure will."

"No, it's okay. I just wasn't expecting that. I need my bag, though. I've got sleep clothes I can change into in it," I said, moving from the rug to the left side of the bed.

He smiled and went to get my bag. I pulled off my boots for the first time in days and set them at the end of the bed. I wiggled my aching toes and smiled at my cracked red toe nail polish. I was lost in thought, staring at my toes, when Dougie reappeared. He sat down on the bed next to me and dropped my bag on the floor.

"I think this is the first time in 18 years that I've ever seen you without those boots on," he said laughing.

I laughed, too and looked at him. He was smiling at me, and I felt myself become shy for some reason.

"I have a confession to make," I said suddenly.

"Let it all hang out," he said, leaning back on his hands.

"I'm stuck on you."

For some reason that simple confession caused his hands to give out from under him and he almost tumbled off of the side of the little fold out bed.

I couldn't help but giggle.

"What did you say?" he asked, struggling to get back on the bed. His face was crimson, and I grinned.

I shrugged and grabbed my bag. I casually walked past Dougie, but he grabbed my arm and stopped me.

"What would you say if I told you that I've been stuck on *you* for twelve years?" he asked.

"I'd say you're jiving me," I replied with a small smile.

He got to his feet and looked down at me. Dougie draped his arms around my shoulders, his eyes smiling, but his face was serious.

"I guess time will tell," he said thoughtfully.

I fell asleep that night with my head on his chest, my arm around his waist, and feeling safer than I had in years.

Five

The next morning, we walked to school hand in hand. And even though the night before we admitted to each other about being stuck, I didn't think of it as anything other than holding hands with my best friend.

"Hey, I've got a question for you," Dougie said as we approached the corner. I watched the cars go by and glanced at the red light before looking at him.

"What's up?"

"Well," he said, shifting his bag on his back, "considering I'm older than you, and considering that I never stayed back, how is it that we're in the same grade?"

"I may have told a little white lie when I enrolled," I replied with a shrug.

Dougie laughed and gave my hand a squeeze. The light turned green, and we crossed the street, the early morning traffic of Baker City being the soundtrack of our walk.

We got to school about ten minutes later. Doug led the way to the grassy knoll by the football field where his friends (and mine) were hanging out.

"Hey Jellyfish!" Bev called out and waving. Peggy, who was standing next to her, gave me a big smile.

"Hey Bev!" I replied with a smile.

"We've been waiting for you! Let's go," she said, looping an arm in mine.

Dougie leaned down and kissed me on the cheek as he went over to join his dude friends and I left with the girls. Where we were off to, I had no idea, but I just let them lead me away nonetheless.

"So, it's pretty rad that you're such good friends with Dougie," Peggy said casually.

"He was my best friend when we were kids. I think his family lived in a different town, and my parents met them at a festival of some sort. Anyway, they came over one day for a backyard BBQ and brought him with them, and I gave him a hug and told him that he was my new best friend. We stuck together ever since," I said with a shrug.

I felt a small smile starting to creep across my lips at the memory. Seeing little Dougie eyeing me suspiciously while I watched him through narrowed eyes was how we first met. Our parents stood by, watching us to see if we would interact while we sat down in separate corners of the backyard, watching each other. When I saw him push his curls out of his eyes, I remembered smiling widely and rushing forward to hug him and try to lift him off the ground. Of course, it wasn't as sweet as I let them remember. Dougie pushed me off of him as hard as he could, and I landed on my butt and burst into tears. He instantly regretted what he did and helped me back onto my feet and hugged me while I wailed into his ear. What finally got me to stop crying and declare him my best friend was when he ran over to the fence that closed in the backyard and picked seven flowers and brought them back to me as an "I'm sorry" gift. He told me that I could make a hairband out of them and they would look prettiest if I wore them.

Yup, that was my Toad.

"You look like you're off in another world," Bev remarked when we stopped walking.

"I was just thinking of when I first met him," I replied still smiling.

"You really dig him, don't you?" she asked thoughtfully.

"In a completely platonic way," I replied quickly.

"So, it wouldn't bother you to see him with another chick then?" Peggy asked suddenly.

I shook my head. "No, why would it?"

She focused on something behind me, and I turned around to see what she was looking at. There was Doug with his arm around another girl, smiling and laughing. I felt myself become angry. I felt myself become betrayed. I felt the urge to run starting to swell up inside of me.

I adjusted the straps of my Life Bag, as I had grown to think of it as, and watched them closely. If he kissed her or held her any closer, I would run. He was the only reason I came back; I didn't expect to get stuck on him, and I wanted us to be like we were when we were kids. Just us and no one else.

He must have felt the three of us looking at him because his eyes wandered over to us. He smiled and waved. I nodded in response and turned my back to him.

"Guess that answers that question," Peggy remarked.

"Yeah, listen, I'm going in. I don't know where my homeroom is and I want to be on time today," I replied breezily as I walked into the school, leaving them behind.

I made my way through the semi-crowded hallways to my locker. It took four tries today before I was able to spin the combination the right way. I reached in and pulled out my schedule for the day and the corresponding books for the first three classes. It took me two turnarounds and a teacher to tell me where my homeroom was.

The first warning bell rang five minutes after I was seated in the far back right corner of the room. I had my nose in my biology book as the students began to file into the classroom. I was actually so into what I was reading about cells and growth that I didn't know that Dougie was in the same homeroom. Not until he sat down next to me and pulled his desk against mine.

I looked up at him for a moment before I looked back down at the book. I flipped the page and continued reading when he reached over and closed it.

"It's too early to be such a drag," he whispered with a grin.

I gave him a dirty look and opened the book again. I flipped through it until I found where I had been interrupted.

"What's shaking, Jellyfish?" he asked. I glanced at him from the corner of my eye and saw his curious face.

"I was just thinking of splitting again," I replied with a shrug.

"Why?"

"I don't know. I thought Baker City would bring back good memories, and it did. For about twenty-four hours anyway."

"What changed from this morning?" he asked in confusion.

I rolled my eyes and went back to my biology book. If he didn't know, I couldn't spell it out for him. He closed my book again and took it from me this time. I looked at him angrily and reached for it, but he held it over his head. Since I was boxed in between his desk and the wall, I couldn't really move to reach for it. So instead, I just crossed my arms over my chest and stared at the front of the classroom.

"Tell me what's wrong," he whispered in a serious voice.

"Nothing," I hissed back.

To be honest, I don't think it was just seeing him with another chick. It was that I woke up feeling exhausted and a bit miserable as well.

He leaned over. "B-"

"Good morning class," the teacher said on her way in.

I gave him a triumphant look before giving her my undivided attention. He looked at me through narrowed eyes before he sighed and looked toward the front of the class.

"Mr. Kenison is there any particular reason you're holding Jellyfish hostage?" the teacher asked curiously, noticing my being blocked in.

Doug threw an arm around my shoulder. "It's okay. We're used to being stuck together, aren't we Jelly?"

I shrugged his arm off and put everything I had left into my tired body to scrape his desk back to where it originally sat. The entire classroom burst into laughter, and even the teacher looked slightly amused. I reached under my desk for my bag and got up.

"Homeroom isn't over, young lady," the teacher said sternly.

"It is for me," I replied as I walked out of the room.

As I made my way down the hallway, I could hear her calling my name and telling me to get back in the classroom. Or what? They'd call my parents? Good luck!

I reached the double doors at the front of school and put my hands on the bars. Instead of leaving, I sighed and turned around. The bell rang to signal the end of homeroom, and I decided to go to my next class.

Halfway to Home Economics, I ran into Bev who was giving me wide eyes.

"Doug's going crazy looking for you. He told me what you did in homeroom," she said.

I shrugged.

"Come on, you need to talk to him. He said you told him that you feel like running again, and he's worried that you've already split," she said, taking my hand and dragging me toward his locker.

Peggy was standing with him, looking around the hallways, presumably for me. Doug was sitting on the floor with his head hanging and his shoulders slumped. I almost felt bad for him. Almost.

"There she is!" Peggy exclaimed when she saw me being pulled toward them.

Doug immediately sprung to his feet and looked around. She reached up and turned his face toward us and pointed. He ran over to us and picked me up off of the ground and held me tightly against him.

"I thought you left me again," he said, his voice cracking.

For a moment, I was limp. I didn't hug him back, and I didn't respond. But when he put me down and looked at me, I saw the face of six-year-old Toad bringing me flowers for shoving me away.

I looked down for a second before looking back up at him and pushing his curls out of his eyes.

"I'm sorry. I just don't feel good today."

The second warning bell rang, and Beverly touched my arm. "Are you going to be okay?"

I nodded, and she gave Doug a lingering look before she and Peggy headed toward their classes. Doug pulled me into another hug, only this one was awkward because my face was being crushed directly into his chest and his arms were more of a vice than anything else.

"You have to promise me that you won't leave me again, Jellyfish. No matter what happens, you won't leave me again."

"I can't," I replied, muffled by his chest.

He pulled back and looked at me with serious eyes. Dougie was dangerously close to tears, and we were both dangerously close to detention if we didn't get moving soon.

"I *run*, Doug. It's what I do," I explained. "Now, come on, we're going to be late to class."

"I don't care. I want you to at least promise me that you won't run without telling me why," he said.

54

It was a fair enough request. All I would have to do would be to explain and then split.

"I promise," I said.

Six

I decided to skip Home Ec. It only made sense since I was already so late to the class. Doug decided he'd skip his first class of the day, too, which was US History. So we went out to the knoll by the football field, laid down in the grass, and watched the clouds roll by.

"Is Marfa the only place you've been to?" he asked suddenly.

"No, I've been to four other places since we moved," I replied.

"Where?"

"Oh, let's see," I said, crossing my hands behind my head. "The first place I ran to was Toledo. It only took them three days to find out where I was and drag me back to Marfa. A few months later, I wound up in Chandler. I thought, maybe, if I stuck closer to home than before they wouldn't find me. Well, that only took a week before I was found by the pigs and sent home. Then Durham and Baton Rouge. I actually was gone for almost two whole months when I moved from Durham to Baton Rouge, and that's where I was caught again. I'm hoping that Baker City is the last place they'll look," I said, laughing. "There is one place that I want to see. I could just never make it that far.

"Where?" he asked, rolling onto his side.

"New York City," I replied wistfully.

"I bet that is a *an amazing* place to see," Doug agreed.

And just like that, the most brilliant, outrageous, and probably impossible idea manifested in my mind.

"We should go," I said, sitting up.

"The bell hasn't even rung yet," he groaned.

"No! Not to class! To New York City! Think about it, Toad! You and me loose in New York? It could be such a fun adventure!" I said excitedly.

"Um, Jellyfish, that sounds great, but I'm pretty sure we can't do it," he said.

"Why not? We can do anything we want! We can *go* anywhere we want! Haven't you been listening to me? We should leave tonight! Oh, Toad, please say you'll go with me," I said, dropping down to my knees and looking at him with hopeful eyes.

Doug shook his head and sat up. "It's not that simple."

"Actually, it is. And you made me promise to tell you when I was going to run next; this is it. I'm leaving tonight after your parents go to bed. I have a little bit of money saved. If you change your mind, which I hope you do, then you can come with me. If you don't, then you'll know where I'll be. You just have to swear to me that you won't rat on me. Not to your parents or anyone else," I said, holding up a pinky.

He looked worried and positively sick. I moved my hand closer to him, putting my pinky eye level with him, and he looked away before looping his in mine and we shook. I'd come back to Baker City eventually. I had just been trying to get to New York for such a long time, and telling Doug about it lit the running fire inside of me again.

"Hey, can I ask you something?" I said.

He nodded.

"Who was that chick you had your arm around this morning?"

He looked confused for a second before a look of understanding washed over his face, and he laid back down, grinning.

"Is that why you were such a bummer this morning?"

I sat down on the grass again and rolled my eyes. He was killing my buzz about going to New York by figuring out why I was so mean to him earlier. Instead of answering, though, I pulled a clump of grass out of the ground and threw it at him.

"It is, isn't it!" he said, laughing triumphantly and brushing the grass away. "She's just a friend, Jellyfish. I'm pretty sure I'm allowed to have friends, right? Male or female?"

"How good of a friend?" I asked casually.

"Nowhere near as good as *you*," he answered, pulling me back down onto the grass. "Is that the reason you want to head off to New York, too?"

"No," I replied, shaking my head. I shifted my body so that the back of my head would rest on top of his chest and stretched my legs out in front of me. We looked like a capital T depending on which way you were looking at us. "I've wanted to go there for *years*. That's why I'm going."

Dougie draped an arm over my waist and sighed. I placed my hands onto his and watched the clouds going lazily by. I smiled as I wondered what the clouds looked like in New York. They looked different in Marfa, Toledo, Durham, Baton Rouge, and Baker City, so I knew they'd look different there, too.

It was going to take days and days of hitchhiking to get there, but it was going to be my best adventure yet. *Maybe I can find a place to live. Maybe I can get a good job, make some decent friends, and hide from that night in Marfa. Maybe I can tuck it away in the back of my mind and be happy for the rest of my life.*

"Um, excuse me! What are you two doing over there?"

I sat up immediately. That was the voice of authority, and even though I didn't know whose it was, I knew we were most likely in trouble. By the way he was dressed, I assumed he was the Phys Ed teacher.

"Well? What's going on here?" he barked as he crossed his arms over his chest.

I glanced back down at Doug, who gave me a wink. He got to his feet and pulled me up off of the grass before answering.

"I think the best way to learn about nature is to be out in it, don't you, Coach? I mean, why *go* to US History when it's happening all around us?" Doug asked.

He had a good point. So good, in fact, that I had to lean down and start plucking the grass off of my dress to hide my smile.

"Get to your classes now or *you'll* be history," Coach warned angrily.

Doug rolled his eyes and took my hand once I had secured my bag onto my back.

"They can be such fascists around here," he muttered as we walked toward the school.

"It's like that in every school I would imagine," I replied dryly.

We reached the double doors to the back of the school and Doug reached for them. He didn't open them right away, though, instead, looking at me for a moment.

"Do you really think so?" he asked.

"Probably."

"Maybe we should test that theory?"

I tilted my head to the side and waited for him to explain. I saw a smile starting to appear on his lips, and I felt a small flicker of excitement deep inside of me.

Maybe…

He leaned down and pushed my hair behind my ear and whispered, "I've heard that New York is beautiful in the fall."

I let out a happy squeal and jumped up on him. Dougie laughed and wrapped his arms me as tightly as I had my legs wrapped around him.

"Tonight?" he asked softly.

"Tonight," I confirmed.

Doug pulled away for a moment and looked at me with a big smile. I knew that he trusted me when I said that this would be a worthwhile adventure. I knew that he was taking a big risk by leaving everything behind to go with me.

I used both of my hands to push his hair back from his face and tilted my head.

"I love you, Douglas Kenison."

He threw his head back and laughed. Even when we were kids and I would tell him that I loved him, he would laugh. It never hurt my feelings because that was just his genuine reaction.

"I love you, too, Jellyfish," he said with a sparkle in his eyes and a grin on his handsome face.

I nodded once, and he put me down. We walked back into the school hand in hand, knowing that tonight would be our last night in Baker City.

Seven

It was almost half past midnight when Dougie and I made our way quietly up the basement steps. I put a finger to my lips when we got to the door. I placed an ear against it, and when I was satisfied that his parents weren't anywhere on the main floor, I put my hand on the doorknob and slowly started to twist it open. I pushed the door gently and it started to creak loudly.

"Shit," I mumbled under my breath.

"Step to the left," Dougie whispered. I did as he asked, and he slid a hand under the door near the hinges and instructed me to push the door open.

It didn't make any noise after that, and I gave him an impressed look. He grinned in response, and we quietly made our way through the kitchen. We moved quickly and were out in the night air a few seconds later.

"Sneak out much?" I asked once we were safely outside.

"No. Not at all. I just hate that damn door creaking so I figured out how to stop it," he replied with a chuckle. "Well, we're outside. Now what?"

"We take Route 86 until we get to I-84. Then we'll see if we catch a ride," I replied, walking quickly.

"You say that like you've done this before," he teased, taking my hand as we walked toward our first destination.

I giggled as we walked the almost deserted streets of Baker City. I knew that it would probably be harder to find a ride at this time of night, but if we hadn't returned from school, his parents would have most likely called the pigs. And the pigs would've shipped me back to Marfa.

After my last great escape, my parents warned me that if I left again, when I came back, it would be straight off to reform school. Since I was pretty sure there was no way I could break out of there, I decided that the last time I ran from Marfa would be the last time they would see me ever again.

I didn't hate them by any means. I was just sick and tired of making them sick and tired. They shouldn't have to worry so much about a kid like me, so I made the decision to spare them. The day would come where I would finally have my head on straight and that would be when I would contact them.

We found our way to Route 86 rather quickly since it ran through most of Baker City. Dougie asked when we should start hitching for a ride, and I told him not until we reached the interstate.

Since I couldn't remember Baker City much, we got a little lost on the way there. But eventually, we found it and started to walk along the highway, thumbs out, hoping for someone to stop. We probably had walked another five miles along the side, when a van pulled over.

"Where ya headed?" a young man asked, leaning over the passenger seat.

"New York City, but we'll go as far as you can take us!" I replied.

"Hop in! I'm heading in that direction. I'll get you as close as I can to Idaho as I can."

I opened the back passenger door and climbed in. Dougie had practically tackled me to get in with me and protectively put his arm around my shoulder. I could see the nervousness in his eyes as he watched the driver carefully.

"What's wrong?" I asked him quietly.

He pulled me closer against him and nodded toward the driver. I smiled; he was afraid that this guy might do something to us.

"What's your name, man?" I asked the driver.

"Travis. What's yours?" he asked, glancing in the rearview mirror with smiling eyes.

"I'm Jellyfish, and this is Toad," I said, putting a hand on Dougie's chest.

"Her boyfriend," he added pointedly.

"That's cool! Groovy to meet you guys," Travis said, nodding.

I glanced up at Doug who was still staring at Travis. I used my forefinger to tap his chest and get his attention. *My boyfriend,* I mouthed questioningly.

He gave me a small smile and pulled my arm around his waist. I rested my head on his shoulder and sighed. I had been so tired lately, and lying against him felt so relaxing.

"So, why are you guys headed out to New York?" Travis asked.

"Jelly's never been. Neither have I. It's just something she's wanted to see for a long time, so I thought we should go," Doug replied, finally taking his eyes off of Travis.

I fell asleep against Doug while he talked to Travis. When I woke up the next morning, I found that the car had pulled over on the side of a field, just off of an exit ramp. I pushed against Dougie's chest gently as to not wake him and glanced out the window. It looked like a beautiful, warm day, so I opened the door as quietly as I could and stepped out.

I stretched and gently closed the door behind me. I walked around the car and leaned on the wooden beam fence that kept the property enclosed. The sun hadn't quite risen fully, and I knew it would be a beautiful thing to watch.

I smiled as dawn started to break over the horizon. It was so pretty that I kind of wished I could reach out and touch the topaz, golden rays. I suddenly felt like a child again and sat down on the wooden fence so I could take my boots off. I placed them by the side of the fence and climbed over.

I ran as fast as I could. I chased the sunbeams as they started to light up the green, green grass. I was happy again; for the first time in a long time, I was genuinely happy again.

The faster I ran, the more I felt like the past didn't happen. Like I was never at that raver that night in Marfa, like I had never decided to take that hit, and like *he* had never forced himself onto me.

Having the mere thoughts float so quietly through my mind was enough to make me stop running. I fell to my knees and gripped two handfuls of grass tightly. I felt the angry tears star to pool in my eyes. My parents had told me to stay home that night but I snuck out anyway. They never knew what happened to me; no one did. I had carried that night with me alone and in secret for two years.

I pulled the grass out by the roots and angrily tossed both handfuls at the sun. But it just didn't seem like it was enough. I grabbed two more handfuls, got to my feet, and tossed them so hard that I wound up falling onto my ass.

I watched the sun set the horizon on fire with color. I wanted that. I wanted to be set on fire with life, love, and happiness. But instead, I was broken, so desperately broken that I knew no one would ever be able to fix me.

"Hey! JELLYFISH!"

I head Dougie yelling as he ran toward me, but I didn't turn to look at him. I couldn't let him see my face or he would know. I was sure of it.

I got to my feet unsteadily and wiped away the tears and frustration before he finally reached me.

Doug spun me around, and I looked up into his eyes. I smiled as much as I could when I noticed his lips were twitching.

Does he really find this funny?

"I'm sorry, Jellyfish. I can tell something is bothering you, but if you could see the dirt streaked all over your face, you'd find this as funny as I do," he said, laughing.

"Huh?" I asked in confusion.

"Oh, you just remind of the time I pushed you into the dirt," he grinned mischievously.

I started to laugh despite myself. I remembered the angry little boy that was mad that I had hugged him and pushed me away so he could "wipe the cooties off of his face."

I put my face against Dougie's chest and wrapped my arms around him tightly. I never knew how much I missed my best friend until I got to spend this time with him. I didn't care that it had only been a few days so far; it was enough to start making my heart whole every time I was near him.

He sat down on the grass and pulled me down next to him. I leaned my head on his shoulder, and he put an arm around mine while we watched the sun come up that morning.

Eight

An hour after the sun rose, we were on the road again. Travis had come over and asked us if we wanted to keep going, and we jumped at the chance. From my prior experience hitching, usually once they pulled over and stopped, you would have to find a new ride.

Doug asked Travis what his story was and that occupied the conversation for the next few hours. Apparently, Travis was eighteen years old, like Doug, and had been driving his way across the States before going to college. He said he had made it back and forth once already and he was on his last leg home. He also told us how he was thinking of going to Canada for a while before going back home to Michigan. (It made sense now that he said he would take us as close to the state border as he could. At any moment, he might just head north.)

listened quietly from the back seat, half lying down, and half leaning on Dougie while they talked.

I had almost fallen asleep again when he mentioned that the real reason he was heading to Canada was because he was sick and his doctor's didn't know what was wrong with him.

"What did they tell you is wrong?" I asked curiously.

"Something is wrong with my immune system and blood cells, I guess," he said with a shrug.

I pulled away from Doug and sat up. It was the same thing I had heard when I had gotten sick with pneumonia once.

"And the doctors in Canada? They can fix what's wrong?" I asked hopefully.

"I don't know, to be honest. But they work free there if you're a citizen, so I plan to apply if I decide to go. I just get so tired, and I don't know if I can make the drive, which is why I've been driving back and forth across the states. To see if I can make it," he answered.

I looked out the window and bit my lip. I wanted to talk more to Travis about his sickness and ask him if I could go to Canada with him. It would be worth a try, even if it didn't work, but I didn't want to have the conversation in front of Toad. He would ask too many questions, and I wasn't ready to tell him yet.

"You okay, Jellyfish?" Doug asked me curiously.

"Yeah, I'm fine," I replied quietly.

I leaned my head back against the seat and looked out the window. I watched the city go by in a blur as we neared the Idaho border.

"Any chance we can get a ride closer to Wyoming?" I asked Travis.

I reasoned that since we were nowhere near the Canadian border, he wouldn't have too much of an issue with it. I glanced toward the rearview mirror and locked eyes with him. He was silent, but his gaze told me he was curious and willing.

"Sure," he said, nodding.

I gave him a small smile and turned my attention out the window again. Doug reached over and put his hand on mine. I glanced at him, smiled at the curious look on his face, and shook my head slightly. With as much as I wanted to trust him, I wasn't sure if I could yet, and that bothered me more than being sick. Not knowing if I could trust my Toady.

Two and a half days, and a boatload of stops later, we pulled into a small diner in Omaha. The bubbly waitress led us to a booth overlooking the highway, and I sat with my head on the window. I had been more tired this morning than ever before, but I brushed it off to not having slept in a bed in days.

As usual, Travis and Doug were engrossed in their conversation. I took a sip of my ice water and made a face.

How can water taste so bitter?

I put the glass back down and continued to watch the cars go by. A moment later, Travis excused himself to the restroom and Doug scooted closer to me. He put an arm around my shoulder and pulled me close to him.

"What's wrong, Jellyfish? And don't try to jive me; I know something is wrong," he said.

I sighed and closed my eyes for a moment. I wanted to jump up on the table and scream that I didn't know what was wrong, that no one did. But he didn't know that I was sick to begin with, and that wouldn't have been fair to him.

"I'm just tired," I replied, glancing at him.

"So tired that you're not eating?" he asked, looking at my full plate questioningly.

I folded my hands in my lap. Even though I had my fair share of good days and bad days, this was definitely one of my worst. I figured now would be as good a time as any to tell him.

"Dougie, there's something I have to tell you," I said quietly.

"So tell me," he said encouragingly.

"Well. A couple of years ago, I was—"

"You guys about ready to go?" Travis asked, reappearing at the table.

Doug looked up at me for a moment before turning his attention to Travis, "Actually can you give us a couple of minutes? I want to make sure she eats something before we go. We'll be outside in five."

"That's cool," Travis said with a nod. "The bill's already been taken care of. I'm gonna go have a smoke."

"Thanks, man," Doug said.

I looked at my plate and reached for the knife that was placed on the left. Even though the smell of the food was enough to make me sick, I decided I could put some jelly on the toast and munch on it slowly. Doug used his free hand to reach for the other piece of toast. He picked up the knife that I had used and spread jelly on the second slice. I raised an eyebrow, looked at him, and he grinned. I shook my head and smiled as I forced down the toast. I wasn't sure how I was going to eat two pieces, but I couldn't hurt his feelings by just leaving it there. So after, I wiped the bread crumbs off on my dress and forced piece number two down. I turned to face Doug.

"I have to tell you something. A few somethings, but you have to promise that you won't get upset or else I won't tell you," I said softly.

"Okay," he said uneasily. I watched his hand as he started to drum his fingers on the tabletop. Even as children, that was a sure fire sign that he was preparing for the worst. And the worst was what I was about to tell him.

I took a deep breath and looked out the window. "There's a reason that I kept running away from Marfa. A couple of years ago, I went to an all-night rave, and I took a bad hit of acid. I mean a *bad* hit; so bad that I almost immediately passed out from it. I'd never done drugs before but I was pretty sure that wasn't supposed to happen. Anyway, I didn't know anybody there, and I wound up dragging myself to a beat down couch that was in a far corner." (His finger drumming became faster and he cleared his throat loudly.) "I'm still not sure how it happened, and I'll never understand why no one helped me, but there was this guy there and –"

"I don't want to hear any more," Doug suddenly said, getting to his feet. "I get what happened. I promised you I wouldn't get upset, so I think we should just go now."

"Douglas Kenison, you sit down and let me finish," I said in a quiet, stern voice.

He let out a loud, heavy sigh and slid into the booth again. Only, he sat across from me and reached for my hands. He held them gently in his hands and looked at me with sad eyes.

"Since you've figured out what I was going to say, I'll spare you the details. A few months later, I found myself not feeling well, but I never told my parents. They had forbid me from going to that rave, so I had snuck out and snuck back in somehow without them finding out. I *couldn't* tell them what happened, you know? I stayed sick, making up excuses as to what it was when they would see it clearly; the sweating, the pale skin, the doubling over in pain, cramping. Anyway, eventually, I went to a doctor. This was about a year ago, mind you, and I was diagnosed with something 'incurable'. Blood cells, platelets, my immune system, all of them are deteriorating. It's the same thing that Travis was telling us he has. I'm sure of it, Dougie. You know, for a second there, I wanted to ask him if I could go to Canada, too, but this time bomb inside of me is ticking away, and I don't know when it's going to go off. I really want to see the skies in New York City before I go on my greatest adventure. Just once," I said softly.

Doug sniffled and let go of one of my hands. I watched him put a fist to his mouth. I watched the tears flow down his face, and I watched him trying hard to hold in his emotions. Dougie was trying to be strong for me, just like when we were little.

"I don't want you to worry about me. I wanted one more great adventure, and I wanted it with my best friend. Thank you for coming with me," I said, squeezing his hand.

He nodded but didn't say anything and didn't look at me. He cleared his throat and wiped the tears away from his face. I watched new ones fall to replace them, following the same liquid trail down his cheeks. I saw him suddenly wave and nod at something outside, and I saw Travis was standing outside, dangling his keys at us.

"Come on, we have to go," he finally said, getting his feet again. I nodded and slid out of the booth. I started to make my way toward the door when Doug grabbed my hand and pulled me back to him.

I looked up into his heartbroken face and felt terrible for telling him. I had just destroyed my best friend when all I ever wanted for him was to be happy.

He took a deep breath and looked at me seriously, putting an arm around my waist and pulling me against him. I assumed he wanted a hug, so I put my arms around his shoulders. Doug reached up one of his hands and ran it gently down my arm, before leaning down and kissing me gently on the lips.

Nine

Travis told us that he decided to go to Canada after all but would take us as far as Indiana. That way, he reasoned, he would be able to just head north and still get us as far toward our goal as possible.

I hadn't said much of anything since Doug kissed me, and he kept up his usual conversations with Travis. If it was true that when you kiss someone you love that you feel a spark, I wondered in what way I honestly loved Doug because I didn't feel a spark. I felt like a meteor had crashed into me and set my body on fire.

I made sure not to act like it. I didn't want him to love me in a way that we shouldn't love each other. My days were numbered, and I didn't want him to be in love with a dead girl walking.

He apologized after the kiss when I didn't react the way he expected. I didn't kiss him back because I didn't know if that would infect him with whatever was inside of me. He told me that he loved me and hugged me tightly. Then we held hands and walked out of the diner.

I crossed my arms over my chest and leaned against him. I decided the best way to forget what had just happened would be to take a nap and chalk it up to a dream.

As I tried to nestle into Doug's side, he shifted and moved his arm so that he could wrap it around my waist while I slept. I closed my eyes and wondered how it would even be possible to not want to love him in *that* way.

I fell into a restless sleep. I dreamt of being in a wide open field full of sunflowers. I was on one end of it, the way I had been before I got sick. On the other side of the field was Toad, and in the middle was a sickly woman who looked like she was about to fall over. I started to walk toward the center of the field. Not because I wanted to see who was standing there so close to death, but because I was afraid, and I wanted to have Toad near me. He had such a calming influence over me that I knew whatever worried me about the girl in the field would go away if I could just get to him.

My slow, careful walking turned into a power walk before it moved into a jog. I finally broke into a run as I saw the girl looming closer and closer, and I told myself to not look at her as I passed by her.

The faster I ran, the closer she got. Behind her, I could see that Toad running toward me as quickly as I was running toward him. He was yelling something that kept getting carried away by the breeze that was going by. I felt tears of exhaustion sting my eyes as I ran faster than I ever had before.

Just as I reached her, she turned to face me. I instantly stopped running and looked into her horribly sallow face. She had marks all over her body, and her appearance was skeletal. She was a shell of her former self. I wavered on my feet as she stared at me with tears coming down her face.

When Toad finally reached us, she collapsed into his arms. He fell to the ground and held her against his chest. I had never heard him cry like that before; like his heart was irreparably broken, like nothing in the world would ever be okay again.

But why was he comforting *her?*

The breeze died down, and my heart began to race as I could now hear what he was saying. Holding this vision of death in his arms, he said one sentence over and over.

"I loved you so much, Jellyfish."

I woke up with a start. The car had stopped moving, and Travis and Doug were asleep. I was covered in sweat, but I couldn't tell if it was from the nightmare or the sickness that was coursing throughout my body. I brushed my hair back and pulled off my hairband. The flowers seemed to have died sometime during the drive. The petals were fragile, wrinkled, and fell off with nothing more than a touch. Just like the girl I had seen in the dream would probably have done.

I opened the car door and stepped out onto the side of the road. If that dream was a declaration of what I was going to be, then I didn't want to go on any further.

Not on this trip. Not in this *life.* I wanted it all to be over before I became a horribly spotted shell of myself.

I looked down at my cherry-red boots and smiled. The only things I had with me for so long, and they weren't in my dream. Maybe I could beat this; maybe they were the way to live a happy life if I kept them with me.

Maybe you're hoping for more than you should.

I looked up at the stars dotting the sky and inhaled the night air deeply. I then leaned down and pulled my boots off. I held them at eye level for a moment so that I could examine them one last time before I placed them in the backseat with Doug and walked away.

It wasn't right to make him suffer this journey with me.

This was one that I was meant to take on my own.

Ten

I think it was the third week of August. I was sitting under a viaduct, and it was raining heavily. I wore the same dress I did when I left Baker City, and I was thankful for the rain since I hadn't showered in days. I didn't have any money, so I couldn't rent a hotel room to sleep or go into a restaurant to eat anything sufficient.

I spent my days moving and finding semi-decent food in restaurant dumpsters. It was harsh, and I hated it, but my hunger had finally returned, and I needed to nourish my body somehow.

The bottom of my feet were raw, and there were cuts all over them, which I was always careful to do my best to clean up after I had fished around in the dumpsters. I remember the doctor saying that anyone that came in contact with my blood could contract what I had, and I didn't want anyone else to have to suffer this damn disease. Whatever the hell it was.

As I sat there, trying to get comfortable, I couldn't help but wonder if my parents had set out to look for me yet. Every time a cop drove past me, I was afraid they were going to pull over, arrest me, and send me back to Marfa.

I looked up at the sky from where I was sitting, somewhat protected by the concrete mass above my head, and smiled. Even dirty, dingy, and smelly I had managed to hitch my way to Lincoln, Nebraska. I wasn't as close as I'd like to be to New York, but I was going to get there one way or another.

I leaned my head back against the cold stone as the rain began to pick up, rocketing giant raindrops toward the ground. In a weird way, I felt like the clouds were crying for me. I mean here, I was, a week away from turning eighteen, and I was alone, sick, and hungry with nowhere really to go.

That's how I looked on the outside. However, on the inside, I felt like I was happier than I ever had been in my entire life. I was free from authority, I was traveling like I wanted to be, and I may not have had money or food, but I was still rich in adventure and full on the self-love of being brave enough to do this alone. I wasn't going to hurt anyone this way. The only person that would suffer would be me, and honestly, I didn't feel like I was doing too bad.

I took naps a lot more frequently, but that was mainly because once I got to Lincoln, no one wanted to pick me up and give me a ride. I glanced down at my disheveled dress and smiled. I looked like I had run through a hurricane and came out alive.

Sighing happily, I closed my eyes. Today was one of those days where I wished Dougie was here. Just so he could sit in the rain with me. I could see his face now, in the darkness I had let myself sink into, with a big smile, holding his hands up to catch the raindrops and probably throwing a small handful of it at me.

I miss you, Doug, I thought, feeling sadness for the first time since I had ditched him somewhere in Wyoming.

I was awoken by someone shaking me. The rain had stopped and the sun was starting to fight through the clouds, making me wince as I struggled to open my eyes.

"Hey, are you okay?" a female voice asked.

"Sorry," I said groggily, "I guess I fell asleep. I'll keep moving."

I figured it was a cop. Those were the only people who would shake me awake and ask me if I was okay.

"No, it's okay. I was just making sure you were alright."

I finally opened my eyes and stared at the statuesque beauty that was hunched in front of me. She was easily as tall as Dougie and had wild brown hair and big brown eyes. She had thin lips, and her heavy-make-up covered face was looking at me in concern.

"I'm fine," I said, pushing myself up to my feet.

"Come on. Let's go to that diner and get something to eat," she said in a kind voice.

I raised an eyebrow suspiciously, wondering how she knew I was hungry.

"I promise I won't bite," she added. "My name is Kimber. What's yours?"

"Jellyfish," I replied.

She laughed lightly as we waited to cross the street. Then she led the way with me following closely beside her. When we got to the door, I almost fainted from the smell of all of the fresh food coming from inside.

I wrapped my arms around myself while we waited for a waitress to come over and looked around the diner. I was definitely being stared at by some of the patrons, and I couldn't blame them. I'd stare too if a dirty, disheveled, smelly, teenager walked in, too.

"Don't worry about them," Kimber said to me quietly. "They're staring because they're jealous."

Of you, perhaps.

But I just smiled at her and kept the thought to myself. When the waitress finally appeared, she gave Kimber a bright smile, which faltered when she saw me standing next to her.

"Two?" she asked with a tight smile.

Kimber nodded then motioned for me to follow her. The waitress put us as far back as she possibly could in the corner of the diner. When she handed us the menus, I dropped mine out of excitement. I was finally going to eat real, fresh, cooked food.

"Sorry," I mumbled, reaching for it.

She gave me a dirty look and asked if there was anything we wanted to drink.

"I'll have water," Kimber said, looking at her menu.

"Um, a Coke, please?" I said quietly.

She jotted down our drink orders and asked if we wanted time to look over the menu, to which Kimber waved her away in response.

"Order anything you want, kid. It's on me," Kimber said, glancing over the top of the menu.

"Really?" I asked.

She smiled and nodded. I looked at the choices and wanted one of everything, but I wasn't going to be frivolous with someone else's money. I wasn't going to repay her kindness by being greedy, so I settled on a double cheeseburger with the works. I double-checked to make sure that the fries wouldn't be extra and put the menu down.

The girl came back with our drinks, and I practically snatched it from her. I stuck the straw in and pretty much inhaled my soda. She stood there, staring at me before she rolled her eyes, grabbed the empty glass, and walked away with it. When she came back with a full glass, I apologized.

"Can we have a new waitress? Preferably a male? I don't like the way you're treating my friend," Kimber said sweetly when she returned.

The young girl looked outraged for a moment before she gave us another tight smile and walked away. Moments later, a young man with big, bright-blue eyes, light brown hair, and a smile that almost made me melt in my chair showed up.

"Hello ladies. My name is Nate, and I'll be taking care of you from here. What can I get you to eat? Or do you need a few more minutes?" he asked kindly.

"I would like the caesar salad and if you would please bring us some bread?" Kimber replied, handing him her menu.

"And for you?" he asked me.

"Double cheeseburger with everything please," I said softly, handing him mine as well.

"I'll put that right in for you and I'll be back with some warm bread rolls," he said, tucking the menus under his arm and walking away.

"He's cute," Kimber said conversationally.

I shrugged and took a sip of my soda. There was no denying that Nate *was* cute, but he was no Dougie.

"Get his phone number," she said, grinning at me.

I looked at her in shock for a moment, but the look of enthusiasm on her face was so grand that I couldn't help but giggle.

"I don't think he would be too impressed with a sick, smelly, homeless girl," I said once my giggles subsided.

"You don't know much about men, do you?" she asked, tilting her head to the side and grinning even wider.

"Not really," I confessed.

"Got anyone back at home?" she asked, sipping her water.

"No. Just a really amazing best friend that I ditched somewhere in Wyoming," I replied, balling up the straw wrapper.

"So, did it just not work out or did you two not jive together?" she asked curiously.

"It was never like that," I replied quickly. "He's just been my best friend since I was five and he was six. My family moved away for a while, and I went back to find him. I missed him, you know?"

I didn't know why I was opening up to Kimber as much as I was. The only thing I could reason was that I was lonely and she was the first person that had been kind to me in weeks.

"Here you go! Fresh bread!" Nate said, suddenly reappearing.

I immediately and instinctively reached for a roll and shoved it in my mouth. Then, I reached for another one, swallowed as quickly as I could, and did it again. I looked up at Kimber who was smiling at my puffed cheeks full of bread. I glanced at Nate who had his somewhat muscular arms crossed over his chest, watching me with a kind smile.

"I can bring a basket just for you, if you want," he offered. "I won't charge you for it."

I had another hand on a roll and was still trying to chew the bread that was in my mouth. I looked hopefully at Kimber who laughed and nodded at Nate. He walked away and came back with another basket. I pushed it toward Kimber and pulled the basket I had half eaten toward myself. She picked up a knife, cut a roll open, and gingerly spread bread on it. I watched her, feeling like a bit of an animal for eating like I was.

"Don't feel bad! If I hadn't eaten in as long as you haven't, obviously, two baskets wouldn't be enough for me!" she said, taking a bite of her roll.

I smiled gratefully and ate two more rolls before Nate reappeared with our food. I leaned back in my chair for a moment, took a deep breath, and then reached for the ketchup bottle and slathered my burger and fries in it.

I devoured the French fries in almost no time. Then, I cut the burger in half and began to slowly eat it. I wasn't sure when I was going to get the chance to have another meal, so this much I wanted to savor.

Kimber quietly ate her salad with minimal dressing as she flipped through a magazine she had pulled out of her enormous designer bag. With as big as it was, I was surprised that I was just now noticing it.

I took a sip of my soda and rested between halves of the burger. Kimber glanced up at me and smiled.

"Do you think you can do this?" she asked, tapping a page of the magazine.

"Do what?" I asked.

"This," she said, setting down her fork and holding up the magazine.

I reached over for it and looked at the pretty blonde girl in the pretty blue jeans and the pretty, white, flower-patterned loose top.

"I don't get it," I admitted after looking at the picture again.

"Model, silly!" she said with a laugh.

I stared at her for a moment. How hard could it be to stand there and have your picture taken?

"I don't know, I've never tried," I replied, handing her the magazine back.

She slid the magazine back into her bag and looked at me with a grin.

"There's a reason I stopped to talk to you, Jellyfish. I think now would be a good time to confess it. I'm a scout, and I think you've got great potential. I brought you in here to see if your personality matches that beautiful face. Also, because even if you say no, at least you got something to eat."

I didn't know what to say. I mean it seemed like it could be a lot of fun. and it was a job, so at least I wouldn't be hungry anymore. But what happened when they found out that I was sick? Terminally sick? Would they throw me away?

"Say yes. I promise it'll be fun, and I'll look out for you," Kimber said, leaning across the table and taking my hand in hers.

I bit my lower lip and looked away. She had just been good to me and fed me; the least I could do was try.

What was the worst that could happen?

Eleven

DOUGIE

A few years passed since I had last seen Jellyfish. The first year I spent trying to find her in every state I could on my way toward the east coast, and the last year I had moved to New York City, hoping that I would eventually run into her. It didn't happen; this place was so big that I never saw the same person twice.

As it was, I had gotten a part-time job doing some auto body work in a local shop, so I didn't have much time to people watch. On the days I was home, I would sit near the open window of my third floor apartment and glance at the people going by. I knew in my heart that she had made it here; it was just a matter of *finding* her.

Tonight, I was lying on my couch watching *All in the Family* when someone knocked on my door. I sighed, shoved myself off the couch, and walked over to the door. I glanced through the small hole before I curiously undid the chain lock, pulling the door open.

"Yes?"

Two of my neighbors were standing outside my door, dressed to impress, holding a neon pink flyer.

"There's a huge party going on at the Copacabana. You should come since you have a night off," the girl said.

I took the flyer from her and examined it. I could tell by the way this was detailed that this was really a rave in disguise.

"I'll think about it. This an all-night thing?" I asked her even though I knew the answer.

"It sure is, man. Maybe we'll see you there," she said.

"Maybe. Thanks," I replied, closing the door and replacing the chain.

I tossed the bright, thin piece of paper on the table next to the door and went back to the couch. I laid back down, crossed my arms behind my head, and chuckled at the shenanigans of the Bunker family. When the show went to commercial, I walked through the kitchen, toward my bedroom, and grabbed a light blanket from the foot of my bed. On my way back to the couch, the pink flyer fell off of the table and fluttered slowly to the floor. I decided to leave it there as I settled onto the couch to watch the rest of the episode.

My eyelids began to grow heavy, and I was fighting the sleep away as best as I could. It was only eight-thirty in the evening, and if I fell asleep now, I would wake up at three in the morning and be up for the rest of the day.

I turned on my side and shoved the blanket onto the red, carpeted floor. If it wasn't on me, it would be easier to stay awake.

I lifted my head off of the pillow when I heard the hollering and laughter in the hallway. I sat up when I heard the sound of paper being slid under my door.

I went over to the door and scoffed when I saw another pink flyer had found its way into my apartment. I picked it and the other one up and walked into my bedroom. I decided to get dressed and check it out because apparently this was the *happening* place to be tonight.

I pulled on a pair of loose, black denim jeans, a blue, white, and black, plaid button-up shirt, pulled on my dark blue Chucks, and went into the bathroom to comb my hair. I glanced in the mirror as I did it and chuckled. My hair was almost always impossible to tame, but I tried my best before I set the comb down.

Nevertheless, I left the bathroom and grabbed my keys that sat where the flyers were and walked out. Copacabana was about ten blocks away from where I lived, but I didn't mind walking.

It was a particularly cool for a night in July, and I walked quickly. After the first few blocks, I saw a swarm of people across the street heading in the same direction, and I debated going home. I wasn't in the mood for this tonight, but I felt like the flyers would keep coming if I didn't get out and just go.

I kept my head down and walked quickly. When I reached the block that it was on, I saw every last person in line was holding their flyer, and I had left mine at home. I sighed heavily and leaned against the wall. All of this seemed like it was for nothing, and I felt a bit frustrated.

I decided to just go home and started to walk away from the line when a hand shot out with a flyer. I looked up and saw a young man with huge, frizzy brown hair smiling at me.

"Don't go home, man. I had an extra one; you can have it!" he said cheerfully.

I thanked him and went back to my place in line. Twenty minutes later, I was walking through the thickest cloud of smoke I had ever seen in my life.

Some of it was cigarette smoke, but the majority of it wasn't, and I damn near gagged as I navigated my way inside the club. Once my eyes adjusted to the stinging feeling, I looked around and wished I had stayed home.

It looked like the Copacabana had turned into the little brother of Studio 54. There were rows of tables near the back where people were cutting lines and snorting them in plain sight. In a corner at the far end of the tables, I saw some people smoking what I hoped were cigarettes, but I knew better than to continue to hold on to that hope.

I turned around and started to push my way toward the front door when I saw something that caught my eye. There was a group of rather glamorous people sitting at one of the tables, laughing and taking turns inhaling the white lines. One of them, though, was sitting there with her eyes closed and her head leaned back against the leather chair, looking rather limp.

Out of curiosity, I started to walk closer to the table. I was honestly concerned that the heavy-make-up wearing girl was either dead or near death, and everyone around her was so high that they didn't care. I figured that at least I could do one good deed before I left this place and feel better about having come here. The closer I got to the table, the more my heart started to race. Something was wrong and none of them were doing anything about it.

"Hey!" I shouted over the music and laughter as I got closer to them. None of them responded, so I started to wave my hands to get their attention.

Still nothing.

I decided not to bother until I was close enough, and I only had a few more people to walk past to get them anyway.

Finally, I got to their table and slammed my palm down on it to get their attention. They all looked up at me in surprise.

"Is she alright?" I asked them, pointing at the girl.

"Yeah, she's fine. That's just how she is," one of the older guys said. He gave her a shake, and I watched her eyes open widely as she looked around. She ran the top of her hand over her mouth and leaned forward to grab one of the metal tubes, snorting up a white line.

"See? Told you," the guy said smugly.

I, however, felt frozen in place. That girl was the girl that I had spent years looking for. That girl was the girl that used to play with me in the backyard and roll around in the dirt with. That girl was the girl that would walk to school with me when we were kids and sneak into the lunchroom when I was there to eat with me. That girl was the girl that left her Hell in Texas to come back because I was her safe place.

Instinctively, I reached forward and lifted her chin. She looked up at me with yellow, sickly eyes and held out the metal tube; she didn't recognize me. Again.

"Get out of the way," I said to the guy that had been answering my questions. When he refused to move, I picked him up and moved him myself. I leaned down and scooped Jellyfish up in my arms and walked out of the Copacabana.

I was halfway home when she started to tremble. I stopped walking, looked down at her, and saw that her eyes were rolling into the back of her head.

Twelve

I was sitting next to Jellyfish. She was lying in a hospital bed with an I.V. in her arm, and she had been asleep since they stabilized her. The doctor said she had a seizure and that she would okay, just have a bit of a headache when she woke up.

Then he began to question me on how it happened. I told him the truth; I figured it would only help her in the long run even if she got mad at me for telling him.

When he asked me about her medical history, I told him everything I could remember about how she had described her illness.

"What was that?" the doctor asked in shock.

"Um. I'm not one hundred percent sure. I can only tell you what she told me. Something about platelets, her immune system, and some other stuff.

I mean, is she going to be okay, though? Have the drugs done anything to her?" I asked desperately.

"What did you say your name was again?" the doctor asked, peering at me seriously over his glasses.

"Douglas," I replied.

"Do you know where her parents are, Douglas?" he asked gently.

"Um. Not really. I mean, the last I heard they were in Marfa. In Texas. But they could've left by now. She just didn't want to stay there so she left and she came to find me and then I lost her in Wyoming. And … this is what happened to her," I rambled.

A quiet groan escaped her lips, and I reached for her hands. I held them firmly in mine while the doctor watched us carefully before leaving the room.

She groaned some more before trying to open her eyes. I watched her wince and put her hand to her forehead.

"Kimber?" she asked groggily.

I didn't respond. I didn't know who she was talking about, so instead I just squeezed her hand reassuringly.

"Ugh, I don't feel good," she mumbled. I watched her run her tongue over her dry lips and reached for the plastic pitcher of water. I held a plastic cup up to her lips and tilted her neck gently to help her drink it down.

"Thanks, Kimmy," she said, still not opening her eyes.

"Who's Kimmy?" I finally asked quietly.

Jellyfish laughed and coughed before she forced her eyes open.

"Dougie the Ladies' Man," she said, her eyes half open. "It's about time you showed up to the party."

I sat down and stared at her. I can tell by her eyes that she still was high or tripping or whatever the hell it was that happened when you snorted the white lines.

"You're mad at me," she said with a giggle. I raised an eyebrow and crossed my hands behind my head. Jellyfish was so far gone that I didn't know if she would come back. What I *did* want to know, however, is what she was doing inside Copacabana with those people.

The doctor reentered the room and asked me to follow him outside.

"Who's that?" she asked curiously.

"That's your doctor. You almost died last night," I explained quietly as I got up from the chair I was sitting in.

Her hand reached out and gripped my arm tightly. I glanced at her, and for the first time in all of our years together, I saw fear in her eyes. I looked down at her hand and gently peeled it off.

"Dougie, don't leave me here alone," she pleaded.

"I'm just stepping outside. I'll be back in."

Jellyfish whimpered, and I had to swallow the lump in my throat. With as much as I loved her, I was going to have to be tough with her; I knew it. She would hate me for it, and she would run, but this time I would chase her. This time we would run together the entire way or not at all.

"This is highly unusual for me to do, Douglas, but she's in desperate need of medical treatment and she obviously can't consent on her own behalf.

I would like to say we can wait for her parents, but I need to get *some* kind of medication in her system as soon as possible. I need you to act on her behalf and make the decisions for her," he requested quietly.

"Done. Do I need to sign anything?" I asked without hesitation.

The doctor nodded and held out the clipboard he had been holding. As I signed my name, he breathed a sigh of relief and told me they would get her started on the most intense medication they could find.

"Thank you," I said, shaking his hand. He nodded again and left to speak with the nurse that was taking care of Jelly. I went back into the room and saw her sitting up in the bed.

"You should probably be lying down," I remarked quietly.

"I want to go home. Will you take me home, please?" she begged me.

I took a deep breath and let it out in long sigh. I was going to let her down, and she was going to be upset, but she had already let me down by running from me instead of with me.

"Who's Kimber?" I asked for the second time.

"A friend that I made in Nebraska. She's a scout and she got me a few jobs. All I had to do was take some pictures. Plus, she bought me a plane ticket to get to New York. Cool, right?" she asked uncertainly.

"Pictures?" I asked curiously.

Jellyfish nodded but didn't explain because the nurse had entered the room. I raised an eyebrow when I noticed she was wearing a mask over her nose and mouth. When she handed me one, I stared at it for a moment.

"You have to put that on, honey, or you have to leave. Doctor's orders," she said as she set the compartmental basket she had been carrying on the bed.

I pulled the mask over my face and secured it.

"What about me? Do I need one?" Jelly asked her.

"No sweetheart," the nurse said softly.

It dawned on me at that moment that whatever it was that was killing her immune system might be airborne. I reached up and pulled the mask down below my chin.

"Douglas, if you don't leave that on then you'll have to leave," the nurse said firmly.

"I won't wear mine if she can't wear hers," I said meaningfully.

The nurse looked confused for a moment before I saw her eyes melt and she nodded in understanding. I smiled at Jelly who was biting her lip and waiting for her mask.

"I'm sorry about that," the nurse said, returning and pulling the mask around Jelly's face. "I forgot yours because I thought you weren't supposed to have one, but the doctor said I was wrong."

Jelly smiled behind her mask. I could tell because her eyes lit up and she crossed her legs underneath her. She pushed the blankets off of her and folded her hands in her lap while the nurse began to change the I.V. bag and tubing, and I found myself staring at the subtle spots on her arms and legs.

The nurse secured the bag before carefully removing the needle from Jelly's hand. I watched her immediately cover the small drops of blood with layers of gauze and slide the new needle in.

113

She then took the rags with the droplets of blood on them and the needle that had been in her hand and dropped it into a small, hard plastic cylinder in her basket. I caught a glimpse of the label and only hoped that Jellyfish didn't.

It was for bio hazardous waste.

She picked up the basket and quickly left the room with it.

"That was trippy," Jelly remarked.

"What was?" I asked.

"The way she was so careful with everything. It was almost like she was afraid of the things that touched or were in me," she said with a shrug.

"I don't think it's anything to worry about." I hated lying to her, but I needed her to be on track as quickly as possible so I could get her the hell out of New York City. "You don't seem like you're tripping anymore," I remarked.

"Because I'm not. I was just tired and my head was pounding and that was how I sound when I'm tired and hurting I guess," she said with a chuckle.

My eyes wandered down to her bare thighs where the spots were the most prominent. She looked up at me, and when we locked eyes, she pulled the sheets up over her legs before looking away.

"It's because I'm sick. That's why those are there," she said quietly.

"I figured as much. It doesn't bother me, Jellyfish. You don't have to cover up for me," I replied.

She sniffled and pulled the sheets up to her chin. I knew that gesture; I had seen it a lot when we were children. Jellyfish wanted a hug but she didn't want to say that she wanted one. Some kind of woman power thing she always had going. So I got up from my chair and sat on the bed next to her, pulling her close.

"Thanks for not giving up on me," she whispered.

I smiled and hugged her tighter than I ever had in our lives. The truth was that I would never give up on her. I wanted to go everywhere she went, and I promised myself that once I found her, I wouldn't lose her again.

Maybe the six-year-old boy inside of me had come to the surface, but I wouldn't lose my best friend without a fight.

Either she would beat this or we would *both* go down in the end.

Thirteen

Three days later, I got to take her home. She was wearing one of my sweaters, which was so large on her diminishing frame that it fell off of one shoulder and covered most of her thighs. Underneath, she wore a pair of my denim shorts, which were also too large on her, so she kept them up with her hands. She was wearing a pair of my old slip on sandals, and she walked a little funny because of them.

It wasn't a great outfit for her to have left the hospital in, but she got a kick out of it and it did the trick.

I unlocked the door to my apartment and stepped back to let her in first.

"Nice pad, Dougie," she said, looking around.

"No. It's not. But it's what I can afford," I replied with a laugh.

"I like it just fine," she said. Jellyfish let go of my shorts and they fell to the floor. I picked them up when she stepped out of them, and she kicked off the sandals, placing them by the door.

I grinned and shook my head. *This* was the girl I was used to. The girl that didn't care what the world thought of her. I gave her a playful nudge as I went by her and made my way to my bedroom.

I tossed the shorts on the bed and went over to my clean clothes hamper to see if I could find some drawstring pants for her to wear. While I dug around, she snuck into the room, grabbed a pillow off of the bed, and whacked me in the back.

"What was that for?" I asked, turning around in shock.

"Let's see what you've got big man," she yelled, tossing the other pillow at me.

It was obvious that she wanted a pillow fight. I reached down, picked up my weapon, and began to slowly circle her. I knew that one well-placed hit would make me the winner, and she would probably give up.

As I came around the front of her again, I raised the pillow over my shoulder, ready to strike, when she swung hers so hard that I fell onto the bed.

I laughed as she climbed onto the bed and stood over me with a victorious look on her face. She held her pillow up over her head with both hands and gave me a smug grin.

"Say uncle."

I held up my hands in mock surrender, allowing her to let her guard down. When she dropped her pillow, I reached up and grabbed her by the legs and knocked her down next to me. Then I grabbed both of the pillows and stood over *her.*

"That would probably be a good idea for you right about now," I said with a grin.

"There's one thing you're forgetting," she said with a blank face.

"Oh? What's that?"

"That I know where your ticklish spot is!" she replied, gripping me behind the knees and tickling me.

I started to laugh uncontrollably as my knees began to buckle. I fought to stay on my feet because I didn't want to land on her and possibly kill her.

"Stop! Stop! I'm going to fall on you!" I said through hysterical laughter.

"Say uncle!" she shouted, still tickling me.

"UNCLE!"

Jellyfish laughed and shimmied out from underneath me so that I could land without falling on top of her.

"You're an easy man, Toady," she said rolling on her side and looking at me with a grin.

"You cheated, Jellyfish. You know you did," I replied with a laugh.

"Sometimes, you have to cheat to get what you want," she replied with a shrug. I turned to look at her questioningly, but she just smiled and sat up. "We should probably get my prescription filled."

"Yeah. I'll go do it. It shouldn't take me too long. Do you have it?" I asked, getting to my feet.

"I think it's in the shorts I was wearing," she said, crawling to the end of the bed and hanging over. I shook my head in amusement as she reached for the shorts and rifled around for the paper before she sat back up and handed me the paper.

I leaned forward and kissed her on top of the head. She smiled widely in return, and I told her I would be back.

I grabbed my jacket and walked down to the pharmacy a few blocks away. I grabbed a basket while I waited for her medicine and started to look for some groceries. Normally, I didn't care about not having the refrigerator stocked, but now that she was there, I wanted her to be able to eat *something*.

I went to the front of the store and paid for my basket full of bread, eggs, milk, pasta, meat, and other things, and then I went back to the pharmacy and paid for her prescriptions.

I walked out of the pharmacy and started to make my way home. The entire trip couldn't have taken more than half an hour, but I missed her smile already.

It was such an odd feeling, what I had when I was around Jellyfish. I loved her with everything that I was, but I wasn't in love with her. I just knew that I was happiest when we were together, and I wondered if she felt the same way.

I walked up the three flights to my apartment and set the bags down so I could unlock the door.

As soon as I set my hand on the doorknob, it was pulled open, and Jellyfish grinned at the look of sudden shock on my face.

"I could see you coming from the window," she explained with a laugh. "Here, let me help you."

Before I could protest, she reached down and grabbed all three grocery bags, leaving me holding just her meds.

I heard the bags crinkling as she started to unpack them in my small kitchen. I chuckled and closed the door behind me, locking it. I threw my keys down on the table and walked into the kitchen to see her already boiling pots of water and measuring the pasta.

"I didn't buy all of that for you to cook it, you know," I said, leaning against the counter.

"Toady ... just watch the master at work," she said, holding up a measuring cup and peering at it before dumping it into one of the pots of boiling water.

"Right. Here are your pills, *master.* Please take them now. Everything else can wait," I said, holding out the bag.

Jellyfish sighed and stuck her tongue out at me, but she took the bag. She went toward the bathroom, and I followed her. I wanted to watch her actually take her medication and not just pretend she was going to take it. She raised an eyebrow at me when I settled in the doorway, and I looked from the bag to her pointedly.

I had to fight the smile that wanted to appear on my face when she rolled her eyes like the stubborn five-year-old I so clearly remembered meeting. She set the bag on the edge of the bathroom sink and opened it. She pulled out four pill bottles and opened the medicine cabinet. I watched her pull out the cup I kept in there and fill it with water while reading the directions on each bottle.

"Can you open these for me please?" she asked, handing them to me. I nodded and undid the caps, carefully handing the full bottles back to her.

She took the recommended amount of pills out of each bottle into the palm of her hand and tossed them in her mouth. I stood there while she chased them with the water and swallowed. She closed the caps on each of the pill bottles and made a sour face.

123

"Thank you," I said.

"No problem," she replied as she placed the bottles into the cabinet. "Come on."

She pushed me out of the bathroom door and got behind me. Her small hands were in the middle of my back, guiding me from the bedroom into the living room where she gave me a gentle shove onto the couch.

"Stay," she commanded, holding up her hand.

I shook my head and picked up the remote and flipped through the channels while Jellyfish cooked in the kitchen.

Ten minutes later, I heard her cry out in pain. I glanced over and saw her holding her hand just below the wrist with blood pouring from a cut.

"Oh, my God," I said, hurrying over to her. I reached for one of the kitchen towels and covered the wound as best as I could.

"I'm sorry. I didn't mean to do that," she said through tears. "You'll have to throw away the food if any blood got into it. And you'll have to burn this towel, too."

"Let's just focus on stopping the blood. Do you think you need stitches?" I asked, guiding her over to one of the small chairs by the kitchen table.

I sat down across from her and moved the towel just enough to examine the cut. It looked like an honest slip, but how would it be possible to slip almost all the way down to the elbow? I glanced up at her, and she turned her face away.

"You shouldn't be near my blood. It could get you sick," she said tearfully.

"I'm sure it's fine. Stop fidgeting, Jellyfish, I need to get a good look at this," I replied, tightening my grip on her forearm. "How the hell did you manage to go so far down?"

She shrugged, still avoiding my eyes.

"Did you just try to kill yourself?" I asked quietly.

She sniffled and shrugged again.

"Obviously we need to have a serious talk. I just need to get the damn bleeding to stop," I replied.

With a sudden and forceful movement, she jerked her arm free of my grip. I looked at her and was met with an angry look.

"I *told* you not to get near my blood! It'll stop bleeding eventually. I just need you to stay away until it does," she shouted.

"Fine," I replied.

I got to my feet and went into the bathroom to wash my hands. She hadn't bled on me, but I just wanted to take the precaution. I went back into the kitchen and pulled the lasagna out of the oven and placed in on the counter. I cut a large square out and set it on a plate before grabbing some bread and a fork. I went back into the living room and sat down.

I had played a game of wills with her years ago, and I knew there was no winning no matter what was said or done, so at the very least, I decided to eat while she bled all over the kitchen floor.

Jellyfish could be stubborn, but when she got scared enough, she would ask for my help. I just had to wait for that moment now.

Fourteen

The bleeding stopped after another ten minutes. She grabbed bleach from under the sink and cleaned the floor and anything else she could dispose of went into black garbage bags.

"I'll be back," she had said as she left with the bags in tow. She said she was going to the incinerator in the basement to burn everything.

Of course she had said that almost two hours ago and she still hadn't returned. I was left on the couch staring at the ceiling wondering where the hell she could have been and if she had run again.

Another hour went by before there was a knock on the door. I jumped over the top of the couch and ran to it. I yanked it open and saw Jellyfish grinning widely.

"Sorry about that. I ... uh ... ran into some friends while I was out," she explained, giggling.

I looked at her suspiciously and pushed her hair out of her face. Her eyes were glassy, and she kept rubbing her nose.

"Jellyfish! You were getting high!" I yelled angrily.

Her face became dark and she pushed past me into the apartment.

"So what if I was? I ran into Kimber," she replied defensively.

"You're lying! You didn't run into Kimber going to the incinerator. Where did you go?" I asked through grit teeth.

She crossed her arms over her chest and turned her face stubbornly. I could tell that she was going to try another game of wills, but this time I refused to back down.

"Fine. If you won't tell me, and you won't stop doing drugs, then you have to leave," I said angrily.

Her face fell, and she looked at me in shock. I knew what she must've been thinking. That I could so easily toss her aside over something so "small." What she didn't know was that it had already broken me. After I saw the way she looked in the Copacabana, there was no way I would ever survive seeing her like that again. And for that much, I was truly willing to let her leave.

"Dougie, I thought you said you loved me," she said, her lower lip trembling.

"I did because I do. But because I love you, I won't watch you destroy yourself. Either you let me help you through what's going on or leave if you're going to continue. If you choose to leave … I won't be here when you come back," I said quietly.

Jellyfish got to her feet and stared at me. I saw the tears starting to fall from her normally bright and clear blue eyes. I couldn't trust those tears because I wasn't sure what they were for— her drugs or for me.

She came over and stood in front of me. She balled her fists angrily at her sides before she climbed onto my lap and put her head on my chest and began to sob.

I put my arms around her and rocked her. I ran my hands over her hair and tried to get her to calm down. She cried herself to sleep in my arms. Not wanting to wake her up, I got a firm grip on her and closed my eyes.

The next morning when I woke up, Jellyfish was still sleeping. My neck was aching and my back hurt, but I hadn't dropped her in my sleep, so that much I was proud of.

She shifted a little in my arms, but her breathing stayed even. I glanced down at her and smiled. I don't think I had ever fallen asleep with her in my arms before. I placed my cheek gently on the top of her head and glanced over at the clock on the wall behind the TV. I had another three hours before I had to get to work, but first, I wanted to take her out and buy her some clothes. Then I would call my boss and tell him that she would be with me today.

I loved Jellyfish, but I didn't trust her enough to *not* go out and get high. I didn't want to come home to that, and she deserved better for herself.

My eyes were fluttering a few minutes later when the phone rang in the kitchen. Jellyfish groaned and sat up slowly. I couldn't help but laugh at her half-open eyes and the way she opened and closed her mouth, trying to get the taste of morning breath to go away.

"Up, little mama. I have to get that," I said, bouncing her softly on my lap.

She grunted in response and moved from my arms to the couch where she curled up into a ball and fell asleep again.

I chuckled as I made my way to the phone and picked it up off of the receiver.

"Hello?" I asked softly.

"Doug, it's Joe. I was wondering if you'd be able to stay a couple of hours longer today. Mike called out this afternoon," he said grumpily.

"Yeah, on one condition; I have a friend that's visiting, and she's not really familiar with this city, and I don't want to lose her in it. Can I bring her with me today? She won't be any trouble, and I'm pretty sure she'd be excited to help out in any way she can," I said hopefully.

Joe wasn't exactly a "one condition" kind of boss, but maybe if he knew Jellyfish *might* do some work around the shop or office, he'd let her come.

"No!" he barked into the phone. "This is a job, not a babysitting service."

I took a deep breath and nervously chewed my bottom lip for a moment, before I replied.

"Then I can't come in today."

I heard him slap his hand against the desk in anger and started to think of what other shops were hiring in the area. Instead of replying, he slammed the phone down and the line disconnected. I sighed and hung my phone up.

I'd go to work with Jellyfish, and if he didn't want me there, then I would leave. The worst he could do was fire me, which he probably just did, but since he didn't say it out loud, I would act like it was another day at work. Except, I would bring the sunshine with me into the shop.

"Who was that?" she asked groggily from the couch.

"That was my boss. He needs me to stay a couple of hours extra after work today. If I still have a job, that is," I explained.

I watched her sit up and look at me with her tired, curious eyes.

"Why wouldn't you have a job?" she asked.

"Because I told him that I'd like to bring you today. One good favor deserves another, doesn't it?" I asked with a smile.

Jellyfish smiled. "I can't go to work in your sweater and my underwear."

"Well, I know that," I replied, laughing. "I was going to take you out and buy you some clothes first."

She got to her feet and stretched her thin arms over her head before dropping them to her sides. I watched her look down and hold out the sides of the sweater, then look up at me with a goofy grin.

"Actually, if you wouldn't mind loaning me another sweater, a pair of boxers, and a belt, I can save you some money," she said innocently.

I raised an eyebrow at her. I knew what she was going to do, but I wasn't comfortable with it. I let my eyes wander down to her feet and felt triumphant.

"You can't go walking around the city without shoes, though, and none of mine fit you," I pointed out.

"So then all you'll need to buy me is a pair of boots," she replied with a shrug.

I stared at her for a moment, the feeling of triumph deflating quickly.

"Little Toady, never forget that I'm always one step ahead of you. Sometimes two," she said with a grin, walking over to me.

I know; that's what has me worried, I thought to myself as she wrapped her fragile arms around me in a good morning embrace.

Fifteen

We were in the bargain shoe store three blocks away, and Jellyfish had settled on a pair of light brown boots. I was honestly surprised since I had showed her the bright, cherry-red boots that were an aisle behind the one she was in.

"No. I think it's time that I try to make a new me," was her response when she saw them.

I was impressed as much as I was confused. I didn't think there was anything wrong with her that she would have to start herself over, but I hoped that she would also include not doing any more drugs with that.

She was pulling the boots off of her bare feet and putting them back into their box when a woman with a face full of horrendously heavy makeup and wild hair came over to her.

"Jellyfish! How are you?" she said loudly, approaching her.

I set the boots down and watched the woman from where I was. I had a suspicious feeling that this was Kimber; the same Kimber that had hooked *my* Jellyfish on the white lines.

Jelly got to her feet and pushed her hair behind her ears, darting a nervous glance at me.

"Hi Kimber," she said quietly.

So we meet at last, I thought grimly.

I leaned across the top of the display and gripped it tightly. It was taking everything in my power not to reach over and slap her in the face.

"Listen, I've got some new clients that would be interested in modeling pictures. If you're still up for it," she whispered loudly.

Modeling pictures?

Jellyfish shot a nervous look toward me before shaking her head. Kimber raised her eyebrows in surprise before she glanced over to see what Jelly had just looked at.

I nodded seriously at her and she grinned.

"Is this your new daddy?" she asked Jellyfish nastily.

"Excuse me?" I asked angrily.

"Oh, didn't she tell you? She would whore herself in pictures that I would trade for some pharmaceuticals. Make sure you get top dollar for her; she photographs amazingly. Especially when she's doing dirty things in the pictures," Kimber said with a smirk.

Jellyfish put her face in her hands and burst into tears. She ran from the store and left me with Kimber. I walked around the aisle and made my way to someone I could easily classify as the most disgusting person to walk the face of the earth.

"Listen you drug-ingesting bitch," I seethed angrily, sticking my finger in her face, "You stay as far away as you can from Jellyfish. You destroy any pictures you have of her. If I find out that you've done anything but, I'll bury you alive in the junkyard where no one will be able to tell your rotting body from the shit smell that's already on you."

I had honestly never been so angry in my life. Nor had I ever threatened anyone, but it seemed to have worked. Tears began to roll down Kimber's face as she straightened her shoulders up and walked out. To be honest, if she wanted to OD on the white lines, that was *her* business, but she wasn't taking Jellyfish with her.

I grabbed the boots that Jelly had picked out and went to the front of the store to pay for them. The short time that I was in line, I kept my eyes on the large window that she was leaning against. I could tell she wasn't crying anymore, so the possibility that she would run would be minimal.

I exited the store with the box tucked under my arm and went over to Jelly's side. I stuck one of my hands in my pocket while she wiped the tears from her face and took a deep, steadying breath.

When she finally looked up at me and smiled, I could see the shame in her eyes. But I wouldn't chastise her, and I wouldn't make her feel less than human for what she did.

"I do believe these belong to you," I said instead, holding out the box to her.

"Thanks," she replied softly, grabbing the box.

"Come on, kid. Let's get you home and see how those boots look with the *perfect* sweater," I said, throwing an arm around her shoulder.

She smiled at me and let me lead her back to the apartment. Once we were inside, she sat down on the couch and put her face in her hands. I went into the bedroom and looked around for my tan sweater, knowing that it would complement the boots, as well as make her usually bright blue eyes pop.

I grinned when I found it and looked around for my black belt with the silver belt buckle, before I walked into the living room to present Jellyfish with my findings.

She still had her face in her hands and only looked up when I asked her to. She inspected the sweater and belt and smiled softly.

"Thanks, Toady," she whispered.

"Hey, it's the least I could do," I replied with a shrug and sitting down next to her. "Try it on."

She got to her feet and pulled the sweater she had been wearing over her head. Jellyfish was careful to keep her back to me so that I wouldn't "see anything," as she put it. I looked at the small smattering of dark marks on her back and felt the sadness growing inside of me. Whatever it was that she had was getting worse by the day.

139

"You forgot to bring me boxers," she said. She pulled off the ones she had on, and I turned my face away. She was standing completely naked next to me, and it was in such an innocent way that I would have felt like a total chump for looking at her.

"Where do you keep them?" she asked.

I knew that her hands were on her hips and that she had turned to face me because of the reflection of her shadow.

"Third drawer down in the dresser. Take the sweater with you and don't come back out here until you're dressed," I scolded her.

She giggled and leaned down to kiss the side of my head before she gathered the boots, the sweater, and the belt, and disappeared into the bedroom.

Five minutes later she emerged and sat down at the edge of the couch. I still had my face turned away from her just in case, but when she hoisted her booted legs across mine, I glanced over at her.

She was smiling; the genuine Light-Up-The-World Jellyfish smile, and she had a simple red flower in her hair. I sighed happily and smiled back.

For that one moment, I felt at peace. I didn't have the dread of knowing that our time was quickly running out looming over us like a dark cloud. For that *one* moment, it was me and her; Toad and Jellyfish, happy just to be near each other.

"Have I told you that I love you, Dougie?" she asked, her smile turning into a grin.

"Not today," I replied.

"Well, I do. I love you. Yesterday, today, tomorrow, the day after, and forever," she said with a nod.

"Let's go out today. Just walk around and look at the city," I replied suddenly.

"But what about work?" she asked.

"He'll live or he'll fire me. Either way, I don't care right now. I want to walk around Manhattan and show you everything. Depending on how long you've been here, I doubt you've seen more than I have," I said excitedly.

She leaned her head against the back of the couch and giggled at my new demeanor. One thing about me was that when I got excited, my hands involuntarily turned into fists and my eyes would get large and kind of crazy.

"Only if you're sure. I don't want you to lose your job over me," she said.

"And I don't want you to lose your life over my not being here. I'm pretty sure that my reasoning wins that argument," I replied, rolling my eyes. "Now get up and let's go!"

I waited for her to leave the apartment, before I grabbed my jacket from the door, ran into the bathroom, and tossed her pill bottles into the inside pocket.

Sixteen

I smiled at the look of confusion on Jellyfish's face when we went to the parking lot of the apartment building and I opened the door to an old beat up blue truck that I had been fixing.

"Your chariot, my lady," I said with an exaggerated bow.

She giggled and climbed in, pulling the door closed behind her.

"I thought you said you wanted to walk," she remarked when I got into the driver's side.

"I lied."

I reached under the driver's seat, found the key that I had hidden there when I first got the truck, and turned it on. I was glad that I had taken so much time to work on this thing because the next few days were going to test just how good of a mechanic I really was.

I pulled out of the driveway and made my way toward the interstate. I wasn't sure exactly how we were going to get to where I wanted to take her, but I assumed going north would be a good way to start.

Five hours into the drive, Jellyfish finally decided to ask me where we were going.

"How long did you live in New York? I want to know if this is going to be as poetic as I want it to be before I answer that," I asked, glancing at her.

The wind played with her hair, and the way the sun was setting behind her made her look almost angelic. She pushed the stray strands of her bangs out of her face before she answered me.

"About a month. Yeah, it had to be. That's why Kimber sent me to the Copacabana—to celebrate my one month whoreiversary in New York," she said with a heavy sigh.

"I'd actually be quite content to never hear that name again," I replied with a chuckle. "Anyway, I was kind of hoping you hadn't been there long enough to consider that one of your skies."

"No. No way. That place was drug and sex infused hell that I'm only happy to get rid of," she replied adamantly.

"Jellyfish, I'm not saying that I don't have faith in you, but you know that you're going to start wanting the white lines again soon. Just … let me help you when you get the urge, okay? Tell me so I can be there for you," I said carefully.

"Douglas Kenison, don't lecture me. I haven't had the urge, and the only one that I knew to get the stuff from was Kimber," she replied irritably.

"Don't bullshit *me,* Bettie Jo Parker," I snapped back. "It hasn't even been twenty-four hours since you last snorted that shit up your nose and you just saw Kimber this morning. Maybe you haven't noticed, but I'm suffering through all of this with you. Your drug abuse, your illness; you're not the only one dying from it, you know."

Jellyfish was staring at me stoically. It had probably been years since she had someone call her by her real name, and I knew how much she detested it. It wasn't until the day before she disappeared with her parents that she told me why. Apparently she had been named for her grandmother who was a terribly abusive woman to all of her children and grandchildren. To distance herself from that legacy, she had adopted the nickname Jellyfish at an early age.

"Pull over. I want to get out," she said quietly.

I looked at her in disbelief for a moment, but then I skidded over to the side of the road. Because we weren't anywhere near clearing the state line, I decided she could take the truck if she wanted and I'd find a way back. I wasn't going to fight for her anymore if she wasn't going to fight for herself.

I leaned over her and pushed the door open. She looked at me one last time with angry tears in her eyes before she hopped out and slammed the door behind her. I took a deep breath and put the car in drive, ready to pull away from the shoulder so I could take a short drive and calm down, when I heard the sound of something hit the back windshield. I turned around and saw that she was hurling giant clumps of hard dirt at the truck.

I opened the door and jumped out. If I could get her to just calm down and let me leave for a few minutes, then we could talk like rational human beings.

"Ow!" I yelled. She had thrown another clump and caught me square in the chest with it.

"I hate you!" she screamed, throwing another one quickly.

"Jellyfish, stop!" I yelled, dodging the dirt as she started to throw them in rapid succession.

"I hate you!" she screamed again. "If you want to leave me then go! Everyone else abandoned me, you might as well, too!"

I managed to make my way toward her without getting hit again. I restrained her arms at her sides while she screamed on and on about how she hated me.

"You have to be the biggest spoiled brat in the world!" I yelled over her finally. "Stop yelling and listen to me! I am *not* abandoning you. I was going to take a short, five minute drive and come back to give you the truck. I will go to the ends of the earth for you to make sure you get better again if I have to, Jellyfish, but I won't do it if *you won't do it for yourself!*"

I hated shouting in her face the way that I did, but I honestly believed that I had reached my breaking point when it came to her.

She was crying hysterically. I knew it was because I yelled at her, and I wanted to feel bad for

147

her, but I couldn't. She was damn near twenty-two years old and she still acted like a child.

I sighed heavily and pulled her against me while she sobbed. I watched as the sun started to go a little bit faster down over the horizon and wondered how many more days I would have with the broken, used, dying girl in my arms.

"Let's watch the sun set," I said gently to her. I led her to the hood of the truck and climbed onto it, pulling her up next to me.

Her breathing was now gasps as she tried to stop crying. She put her head on my chest and her arm around my waist while we laid there and watched the last few rays of sunlight fighting to hold on to the sky.

"That's what I feel like every day," she whispered shakily. "Only one day, I won't come back up."

"And the world will stop spinning that day. The sun will refuse to shine, and the stars won't light up the night in protest," I quietly assured her.

"It'll all be dead. Just like me," she said softly.

I sighed deeply. The fact that she had just resigned herself to death was the one thing that I had been dreading the most. I didn't want her to give up her fight, and I didn't want a world without Jellyfish in it.

"Dougie?" she asked.

"Yeah?"

"Remember when we were in that diner and you kissed me?" she asked, pushing herself up to a seated position.

"Yeah."

"Can you do it again please?"

I smiled and ran a hand over the side of her face. That kiss had haunted me for the years that we weren't together, but I didn't want to tell her. Now that she wanted me to do it again, I wondered if her feelings for me had changed. I didn't want to ruin her request with questions, so I nodded and leaned forward, pressing my lips gently against hers. Jellyfish's fingers dug into my chest as she pressed her lips back against mine, but when I opened my mouth slightly and tried to gently part her lips, she pushed me away.

"What's wrong?" I asked in confusion.

"I … I just don't know if we can do that without me getting you sick," she replied quietly.

"I'll risk it," I replied reaching for her again.

"*No,* Doug. I wouldn't be able to handle it if you got sick because of me," she said firmly.

I raised an eyebrow at her. "I thought you said you loved me."

"I do. And because I do, I won't let you live with this death sentence," she replied.

"Jellyfish, I started to live with that death sentence when you told me about it in that same diner that I kissed you in. I never told you this, but that kiss was my way of letting you know that we're not only going through this together, we're ending it together," I said softly, taking her hand in mine and placing it over my heart.

She looked at me with fresh tears welling in her eyes. I think it finally sunk it what it meant when I spent the past few days telling her that we were in this together.

"Tell me why, Dougie," she whispered.

"Isn't it obvious? I love you, Bettie Jo Parker," I replied with a small grin. "I always have. Since that day that I pushed you into the dirt to the day that I sat on those stairs waiting for you to come home so we could play. From that moment you walked back into my life in high school to the moment where you ditched me five years ago. But I honestly can say that I loved you most of all when I saw you so helpless in Copacabana, and even more now that you're here with me watching the sunset on this beat up truck. We almost started our lives together so it only makes sense to me to be together in the end," I explained with a shrug.

She moved from her spot next to me and sat carefully sat on my lap. I looked into her eyes as she took my face in her hands and leaned down, kissing me gently and slightly devilishly all at once. I wrapped my arms tightly around her waist and returned her kiss. We sat on the hood of the car, entangled in each other's embrace, kissing like long lost lovers, when she finally pulled free.

"Woman, you've got to learn to get that under control," I laughed, reaching for her again.

"I stopped because I can feel it," she said pointedly. I felt my face turn crimson with embarrassment as she crossed her arms over her chest.

"Sorry. Maybe you should get off then?" I suggested.

She smiled and hopped off of the hood of the truck. I let my breath out and closed my eyes. Behind me I could hear her opening the doors and then closing them a moment later. Then I heard her climb into the bed of the truck and call me over to her.

I slid off of the hood and walked around to the back of the truck. I laughed when I leaned over the side and saw that she had made a makeshift bed of old quilts that I had put in the back of the truck when I first bought it.

"This might turn out to be dangerous," I teased, wiggling my eyebrows at her.

"Not if we're careful. I'm not exactly sure how this *thing* goes around, but I've never been with anyone that honestly loved me, and I was kind of hoping that ... maybe just once ... before I died, that I would know what it felt like. It's been my secret wish," she said softly.

I looked at her for a moment, contemplating what she was asking of me. Yes, I loved her, and she loved me, but we weren't in love with each other. The worst that could happen would be that this would ruin our friendship. The best that could happen would be that she would at least have gotten her wish.

"You don't have to do, Dougie. I just know that if anyone in the world loves me, it's you," she said.

That was all I needed to hear. I climbed into the bed of the truck with Jellyfish, and while the sun finally disappeared, giving way to the moonlight, I gave her the one thing she wished for.

Seventeen

We were back on the road when the sun came up the next morning. We drove in a comfortable silence for the first hour until I decided that it was driving me crazy.

"I kind of feel like a genie," I said nonchalantly.

"Oh, yeah?" she asked.

"Yeah, you know. Granting wishes and things like that," I replied with a grin.

Jellyfish laughed and shook her head. "If you're a genie that means I get two more wishes."

I glanced at her and saw the mischievous look on her face and nodded. I knew she wouldn't ask me for anything I couldn't handle or anything that wouldn't be fun, so why not?

"Deal," I said, holding out a hand for her to shake.

"I saw a genie once. Remember that time I told you about that first and last hit of acid I ever took? Well, I saw a genie after I took it," she said conversationally.

I laughed and turned the radio on quietly. I didn't want to hear about that night, but I didn't want to not listen to anything she wanted to tell me. After all, being her best friend made it my obligation to listen to anything and everything she had to say.

"Can't say I've ever seen one," I said, tapping my hands to the beat of the song on the steering wheel.

She giggled and turned the radio up louder. Another hour of silence passed before it was broken by her this time.

"I have to use the bathroom, and I'm hungry," she said.

"If you see a restaurant or something, point it out and I'll stop," I replied.

Twenty minutes later she tugged on my arm and pointed at a diner that looked about a mile away from the exit. I nodded and pulled off of the highway. I stopped at the gas station first to fill up the gas tank before scooting us over to the decently sized diner.

We got out of the truck, and I held out my hand. She smiled and firmly gripped mine as we walked toward the front doors. I held it open over her head and waited for her to go in before I entered behind her.

The hostess led us to a table immediately and our waitress almost appeared right behind her. She was bubbly and super nice, making us both laugh as she handed us menus and made suggestions and *anti-suggestions* as she called them.

"Ah, shit. I forgot your pills in the truck," I said suddenly getting up. "I'll be right back."

Jellyfish smiled and nodded as I made my way quickly out of the diner. I walked over to the truck and reached for my jacket where I had her medicine stashed and read the bottles. I poured out the right amount of each and put them into my pocket. I was sure that she wouldn't want people staring at her for taking the pills out herself, so I spared her that much.

As I made my way back in, I saw her sitting by the window where I left her, but it looked like she was talking to someone. I raised an eyebrow and made my way quickly back inside where I saw a little girl standing next to her.

"Suzie, this is my very special friend, Mr. Douglas. Doug, this is my new friend, Suzie," Jellyfish said, introducing us as I slid back into my spot across from her.

"Hello, Mr. Douglas," the little raven-haired girl said.

"Hi Suzie," I replied with a warm smile.

"Suzie here was just asking me why I have so many spots on my body," Jellyfish explained.

"Did she tell you yet?" Suzie shook her head "It's where the angels have kissed her. They love her so much that every night when she goes to sleep a new one comes by and kisses her to make sure she'll only have good dreams."

"I have angel kisses too!" Suzie said excitedly. She rolled back the long sleeves of her dress and showed us her arms.

Jellyfish inhaled sharply, and I exchanged a glance with her. This little girl, Suzie, had the exact same "angel kisses" that Jellyfish had. She was sick just like her.

"Mommy and Daddy told me that I'm not supposed to show anybody these because then people will be scared of me," she whispered loudly, rolling her sleeves back down.

"We won't tell. Promise," Jellyfish said softly.

Just then a young man that looked exactly like little Suzie appeared and took her hand. He apologized if she bothered us and walked away with her. I waved as she turned and gave us a big smile.

I turned my attention back to Jellyfish who was fiddling unhappily with her straw. I reached into my pocket and took her hand, placing her meds in her palm.

She opened her hand slightly and looked at her pills before standing up and scanning the diner. I watched curiously as her eyes settled on a table clear on the other side of the diner. She walked away without a word and made her way over. I craned my neck and watched her crouch down next to the table. That's when I realized it was Suzie's table, and that Jellyfish was talking to her parents. After a few moments of conversation, Suzie's mother put a hand over her mouth and started to cry as her father nodded at something Jellyfish said.

Suzie got up and hugged her happily before she took something from Jellyfish.

I raised an eyebrow as she walked back toward me with a grin. She slid into her spot across from me without a word and took a sip of her drink.

"What was that all about?" I asked curiously.

"I gave her my meds."

"But you need them!" I said more frantically than I meant to.

"So does she. They can't afford any for her, Dougie. I told them that when they're done eating to come over and you'd take them to the truck and give them the rest of what I have," she said softly.

I leaned back in my seat, my mouth wide open in disbelief. I didn't know how I was going to tell her that there was no way in hell that I would do it. I wouldn't give her meds to someone else, no matter how young they were. Her amount of selflessness was rivaling my selfishness right now; I wanted to keep her for as long as possible, and I wouldn't give up her meds without a fight.

"I won't do it," I finally said.

"Yes, you will, because I *wish* that they wouldn't have to worry about her getting medication for a short while," Jelly said meaningfully.

"*No.*"

"Douglas Kenison, you promised me three wishes. This is one of them. Please give them the rest of my medication when they are ready to go," she said, giving me a level stare.

I took a deep breath and looked down for a moment. I wanted to reach over and shake her, but she was right; I did promise her.

"I'll give you the keys, and I'll tell you where the bottles are, but I can't physically give it to them," I said finally.

"Why?"

"Because I can't knowingly hand over the few things that I know might be giving you extra years of life. But I'll meet you halfway and tell you where they are, Jellyfish. That's the most I'll do," I replied stubbornly.

"Fine, that's a half of a wish, though, so you still owe me one and a half," she replied with a smile.

I took the keys out of my pocket and threw them onto the table. I was frustrated, and it was beyond obvious. But this was what she wanted, and I would do my best to oblige.

"You know, Dougie, I hate to say this, but it's *my* adventure that we're on. If this is how I choose for this road to curve, then you have to accept it," she said quietly.

"Know what I think?"

"What?" she asked.

"That I get the most bogus pieces of news in diners. I'm not stopping at these anymore," I replied, looking out the window.

She laughed, and I smiled despite my mood. It was the truth, though. Five years ago was when she told me about being raped at an all-night rave and getting sick because of it, and now she was telling me that she wanted to give her medicine away. These places were apparently a curse.

Our food came, and as we ate, Jellyfish tried her best to pry out of me where we were going. I wouldn't tell her because I didn't want to ruin the surprise.

I had just finished my roast beef sandwich when Suzie and her parents came to our table. Jellyfish smiled at them and wiped her mouth with her napkin before getting to her feet. After a quick introduction she led them out to the truck where I watched her give them the only things that were somewhat sustaining her life.

I watched her get on her knees and hand Suzie the bottles as she explained the labels to her. Then I watched them hug tightly before she stood up and waved goodbye to them.

I sighed miserably. She was too kind for her own good; especially in this situation where she *needed* what she just gave away.

I turned my face away as the scene finished playing out, and as she walked back toward the diner, looking around for the waitress. I wanted to pay this bill and get out of here before she dropped dead just on principle.

"Stop looking so glum, chum," Jellyfish said as she approached me. I rolled my eyes and shook my head. Not even giving away life sustaining medicine would shake her usually happy demeanor.

"If it makes you feel any better, she made me keep half of them," she said, opening her hand.

"Jellyfish, can I ask you a question?"

"For sure," she replied as she grabbed a napkin to put her meds in.

"Why did you do it? Honestly?" I asked carefully.

She put the napkin in her pocket and looked up at me with a smile. "Because, Dougie, I've lived longer than her. I think she deserves a few more years, don't you?"

I didn't respond. There was nothing I could say to dispute that, so instead, I just asked her if she wanted to take her food with her. I didn't want to sit there any longer than necessary.

Jellyfish pushed her plate away, finished her soda, and followed me out of the diner. When we got to the truck, she hopped in, and I leaned with my back against the driver's side door for a moment.

"Want me to drive, Dougie?" she asked.

I laughed; it never dawned on me that Jellyfish could drive because in moments like this, I still saw her as the five year old with pigtails who was desperately trying to be my friend.

"Can you do it without getting us killed?" I asked, turning to face her.

She stuck her tongue out at me and took the keys from my hand. I walked around the back of the truck and smiled at the quilts still laid out. I bundled them up in my arms and tossed them into the backseat before I got in.

"Where are we going, anyway?" she asked me curiously, starting the truck.

"North."

Eighteen

Three hours later, we saw the sign I had been dying to see. Jellyfish pulled the truck over and started to cry. She finally understood what I was hoping for.

Welcome to Ontario. More to discover.

"I never forgot what Travis said or the look on your face when he said it. I figured the least we could do was try," I said, putting a hand on her leg.

She couldn't speak through her tears, so instead, she leaned across and hugged me tightly. I chuckled and put my chin on top of her head. I left my family, my job, and soon, I would leave my country knowing that it would all be worth it if she would just get better.

"We should probably trade places or we're never going to get in there, cry baby," I joked.

She didn't laugh; she just nodded and got out of the truck, still crying.

I'm going to have a major headache by the time we get through the border, I thought with a chuckle.

I adjusted the seat so that I wouldn't be plastered against the steering wheel and pulled back out onto the highway. Jellyfish was still sobbing uncontrollably, and I was hoping that customs wouldn't think this was a hostage situation of some sort.

The customs agent looked at us suspiciously before asking what our business in Canada was. I explained that we were visiting family and that Jellyfish was so happy about finally getting to see them that she turned into a hysterical mess.

"Get that under control, Parker. It's making us look crazy," I whispered quietly.

The agent stared at her for a moment before inspecting the truck, then waving us through.

She took a few deep breaths and blubbered loudly one last time before she managed to calm down. I glanced over at her and laughed, giving her leg a quick squeeze.

"I don't know if we can get citizenship, but I'll do my darnedest to make sure you get better," I said as I drove down the highways of Ontario.

I was paying special attention to the signs because I had another surprise for her. Something I had come up here a few months ago and did in case I ever ran into her again.

I knew it would make her cry, but I was hoping that she had just spent all of her tears because it was honestly starting to give me a headache. I pulled off Highway 401 and started to drive through the city's streets. I had only made this trip once, so doing it from sheer memory was proving to be a bit of a challenge.

But it only took about five U-turns and half an hour before I managed to find what I had been looking for. I pulled up to the white brick apartment building and looked around for parking spot number twenty-three.

"Where are we?" she asked curiously.

"Home," I replied with a smile.

Jellyfish looked at me with wide eyes, and I watched her lower lip trembling dangerously. I rolled my eyes and sighed; with as much as the

167

crying had become a regular occurrence, I just couldn't get used to it.

"Jellyfish, if you cry again, I'm going to scream," I said.

She sniffled and wiped the tears from her eyes, turning her face away from me.

"Why did you do this, Dougie? I don't know how much time I have left and you … I don't want you to be there when it happens," she said quietly.

"I told you; we have to at least try," I answered, turning off the car and hopping out. Jellyfish was still sitting in the truck, and I leaned in the driver's side window. "You coming? Or do you plan on blubbering for a while?"

She put her hand on the door handle and took a deep breath before she opened it and got out of the truck. I started to fish around in my pockets for the keys to our new apartment when she ran around the front of the truck, spun me around, and hugged me tighter than she ever had before.

I laughed and returned her hug, but my heart felt heavy when I put my arms around her. It was obvious that she was slowly losing weight, and that scared me. I wouldn't show it though, the fear, I had to be the strong one, and I would be.

"You know, I have an idea," I said, resting my chin on top of her head. I inhaled her scent of papyrus and felt my eyes water. How many more times would I have this chance?

"Hm?" she asked into my chest.

"Well, I was thinking … we're best friends, right?" I asked. She nodded and turned her face up to look at me. "What if we decided to kind of do a … thing … like where we promise to stay together until the end and only be with each other? That way you know that no matter what you'll always be loved, and I'll always have my best friend by my side," I suggested nervously.

"Like get married?" she asked curiously.

"No! Not *married,* more like a promise of forever? We can get some groovy rings, but not wear them on *that* finger, you know? I just want to be able to give you everything that I can before –" My voice cracked. The longer I stood there, thinking about her fragile body, inside and out, the more it was becoming a harsh reality that I wouldn't have my Jellyfish as long as she deserved to be here.

169

I had always thought that we would grow up, attend each other's weddings; she would be the best man at mine and I at hers, and that we would live in the same neighborhood. Our children would grow up to be best friends like us, and we would be there for each other when we were old and alone. We'd die on the same day, but we'd die happy knowing that through it all, we had stuck together and kept our promise of being best friends forever.

Twenty-three years we had been together, even though we were apart, and now we didn't have enough time.

Nineteen

A few months later, we finally felt settled in. I found another part time job at a larger chain auto body repair company, and Jellyfish decided to keep busy by babysitting three times a week. I told her that I didn't want her to work, but she said that she wasn't dead yet, and she wanted to contribute as much as she could.

When I came home from work that night, she had dinner waiting on the table where she was sitting.

"Hello, beautiful," I called out as I walked in the door. It had become a customary greeting in the past year. She had lost more weight, more "angel kisses" appeared on her body, and nothing she wore fit her right. But her smile never faltered, and her blue eyes were always brightest when they looked at me.

"Hi Dougie!" she said happily.

As I set my lunch bag down and tossed my flannel jacket onto the couch, she sprang from her seat and grabbed a plate.

"I made garlic roasted mashed potatoes, a pork roast, and fresh bread," she said as she began to load a plate for me.

"Wow. Thanks!" I said appreciatively as she set the plate in front of me. She went back to her seat across from where I was and pulled one of her legs up onto the chair.

"How was your day?" she asked.

"Busy. I did one damn thing today and that was rebuilding a carburetor," I replied, shaking my head. I grabbed the fork that had been sitting to the left of the setting and dug into the mashed potatoes.

She smiled and reached for a napkin. She coughed a couple of times into it and then got up to throw it into a plastic bag. I hated those plastic bags; they were everywhere, and if she coughed, sneezed, or bled on something, she would throw it into separate plastic bags so she could dispose of them on her own.

"So, what did you do today? Besides make this amazing dinner?" I asked, using my knife to slice a piece of the roast off.

"Well," she said with a mischievous grin. "While I was out shopping, I happened to pass a really gnarly shop, so I went in and had a chat with some of the guys there. Wait until you see what I bought!"

She ran away from the table excitedly, and I sat there curiously picking at my bread. I hoped that whatever it was wasn't expensive or a waste of money, but I wouldn't reprimand her either way. If it made her this happy then I would live with it.

A couple of minutes later, she came back to the table holding a big box. She set it on her chair and pushed her hair out of her face as she reached in and pulled out some kind of contraption.

"What the hell is that?" I asked.

"It's a tattoo machine!" she replied excitedly.

I dropped my fork and rubbed my forehead, taking a deep breath, "Jellyfish, what do you plan on doing with that?"

"Me? Nothing. I'm just going to sit here. *You* however, are going to cover up these hideous marks on my body with this," she said, holding it up.

I looked at her like she had lost her mind. I had never in my life used a tattoo gun before, and I didn't even know how to turn it on.

"Douglas, don't give me that look. I remember those pictures you used to draw for me when we were kids. You can put whatever you want on me, as long as we cover these things," she said, pulling off her horribly oversized sweater.

I felt my heart shatter every time I would see how frail she was becoming. Jellyfish was standing there in her bra and my drawstring shorts, which were pulled so tightly around her waist that it was a wonder that they *still* hadn't fallen off. I saw the angel kisses on her right arm more than her left and, I saw the way they were appearing on her belly. Her thighs were starting to show signs of them, too, and I—*God, please don't take her away from me. Please.*

"I'll do my best," I replied softly.

"Good, we can do some tonight after you shower," she said cheerfully.

"Wait a minute. Don't you think I should talk to one of those people at the shop to find out how to do this?" I asked.

"Nope. I already did," she replied with a sly smile. "It seems really easy, Dougie, and I trust you, so I'm not worried about it."

She put the box on the floor and sat back down in her chair. She folded her legs underneath her, cross-legged, and began to give me suggestions for what I could put on her body. Permanently. With ink. And no experience doing it.

"...also, the guys said that if you do a really good job, they'd hire you," she was saying.

"What?" I asked, visions of horrible and permanent stick figures dancing in my head. With big heads and crooked bodies; I probably couldn't even draw a straight line anymore.

"They said they'd give you a job at the shop. They make a lot of money there, I think. I mean, it's *really* nice in there. Do you feel okay? You look like you're going to be ill," she said in concern.

"Fine," I replied with a nervous chuckle. "I think I just want to get this over with. Could you put this in the stove for me? I'll finish it before I go to bed; I'm gonna go put on some comfortable clothes and get a towel or two. And maybe a bucket."

I scraped the chair away from the table and walked into the bedroom. Jelly sighed loudly behind me as she put my plate away and started to clear the table. I grabbed a pair of old gym shorts that I had and a white t-shirt and went into the bathroom to change. I caught my reflection in the mirror and sighed unhappily at myself. I would never do this ever again for *anyone,* no matter how good it came out. This was something that my best friend asked me to do, and I would do it for her and her only.

When I came back into the kitchen, she was sitting there with her hair pulled back into a pony tail, a red flower in her hair, and in her bra and my shorts. She gave me a big grin and waved me over.

"Come on, Kenison! I already put the machine together. Here are some colors and stuff, and here are some directions on how to use it. Also, I bought some gloves at the grocery store that I want you to where. The guy said I might bleed, and I *do not* want to bleed on you," she said, shoving a small rectangle box of gloves toward me.

I shook my head and nervously pulled on the gloves. The left glove got stuck on my ring, and I had to carefully stretch it over it so that I wouldn't rip the glove and send her into a frenzy of tears. Even though I had insisted on not wearing the rings on the marriage finger, she insisted that we did. I let her win that battle because I just didn't want to argue over it any longer than we had. I sat back and read the directions. Seven times. Backward and forward to make sure that I hadn't skipped anything.

"You are one crazy little mama," I said quietly, shaking my head and reaching for the gun. "Did you sterilize the needles?"

She nodded and stood up, bringing her chair over to sit sideways in front of me. I put my foot tentatively on the pedal, and the machine buzzed to life. I sighed and stuck the tip of the gun into black ink, before I hovered over her arm for a moment.

"Are you *sure* you want me to do this? I'll pay for you to get these done, Jelly," I said quietly.

"Yes, Dougie. I just … I want to be pretty when they lay me down in the ground. I want the flowers to grow over me because they aren't afraid that they'll catch something from me that will kill them. I just want to know that when it's all said and done, that no one will ever be afraid to be near me again or look at me differently because I'm sick. I want everyone to look at me the way *you* do; to see me as a girl that was in love with this world and just wanted to make everyone smile. I want the world to know that even though I was sick, it didn't stop me from being happy, that it didn't stop me from doing everything that I could, that I wasn't loved any less, and that I wasn't any less human," she said softly.

"Deep breath, baby doll. And let me know if this hurts too much," I replied, putting the needle to her skin.

I had never worked so hard to make things as perfect as I did that night.

Twenty

Three nights later, I had finally finished drawing all over the pieces of her body she wanted covered, and we were sitting on the couch watching TV. She was bundled up next to me, and I had my arm around her, holding her close.

"I was thinking about something," she said when the show we were watching went to commercial.

"Oh, yeah?" I asked.

"Mhm. I think that it might be safer for the eco-system if I was cremated instead of buried," she said matter-of-factly.

I grunted in response.

"Seriously, think about it," she said, sitting up and turning to face me. "If I'm cremated, you can take my ashes and spread them in the places that I ran to and keep some for yourself."

"I don't want to talk about this," I replied quietly.

"Doug. It's reality. I don't have much time left; I can feel it. I want you to know what I want done when I'm gone," she said.

I sighed heavily and ran a hand over my face. There was something that I needed to tell her, but I didn't want to. Especially since she was so happy and accepting of the fact that I would outlive her. I grabbed the remote and turned up the volume once the show was back on, and she bundled up next to me again.

I had gone to the doctor a few days ago because I hadn't been feeling right lately. He had called me last night when she was in the shower and told me that I was … sick. Jellyfish's kind of sick. That one night that we spent together on the side of the highway on the road to Canada … I had contracted her illness.

With as much as I knew that I shouldn't keep it from her, I refused to upset her. I didn't want her to die thinking this was her fault when I could have easily said no.

On the next commercial break, she poked a finger into my ribs, "Out with it, Kenison. Something is bothering you."

"I just don't want to talk about death and dying," I grumbled. *But I have to sit here and listen to you telling me to cremate your body and scatter you around the United States,* I finished silently to myself.

"Well. There *is* one thing I would like more than anything in the world before I leave," she said quietly.

"What's that?" I asked tiredly.

"I want the barn where the raver was held burned to the ground. I want to see it go up in flames before I have to," she replied.

I leaned my head back and stared at the ceiling. That was actually something I would enjoy doing greatly. Burning down the place that put her through this slow, hellish death would be a pleasure beyond words.

"Just say when," I said.

"How about now? We can leave tonight and get there by Sunday," she said, glancing up at me.

I smiled at her and nodded, getting to my feet. If it made her feel better and if it made the death talk stop for a day or two, I was willing to do it.

"Got to stop in New York City first, though. I want you to see the big city lights again," I replied softly.

"One last time," she said with a smile and a nod.

I had to trust that she knew her body better than I did. If she wanted to see the barn in Marfa burned to the ground, it was because she knew she didn't have much time left. She didn't look any sicker as the days went on, but she moved slower and breathed a little heavier. I knew she was hiding it well, and I wanted to do this one last thing for her. So when I went into the bedroom to pack clothes for us, I found myself sitting on the carpeted floor, struggling not to cry. I didn't want a world without Jellyfish; it wasn't fair, and it wouldn't be right.

I let out a gut wrenching sob and buried my face in my hands. I didn't want her to hear me crying; I didn't want her to know how badly this was killing me inside.

I sat there for about twenty minutes, crying as quietly as I could before I walked into the bathroom to wash my face. I put my hands on the sides of the cold, ceramic sink to steady myself and looked at my reflection.

"Stop crying. You're supposed to be the strong one," I said to myself quietly.

I took a deep breath and walked back into the bedroom to finish packing everything. I grabbed her flower clips and hairbands, making special care not to forget her boots, and went into the living room.

"I think I've got everything," I said, setting it all down in the doorway.

I looked up and saw that the couch was empty; the blanket tossed carelessly on it. I raised an eyebrow and walked toward the kitchen, but there was no one there.

"Where did she go?" I mumbled quietly.

That's when a note on the kitchen table caught my attention. It was folded in half and said "Toad" on the front.

My hands shook as an uneasy feeling washed over me. I reached for the note and sat down.

My Toady,

You're probably going to be mad at me, but when I said I wanted to see the barn burned to the ground, it was because I wanted to go do it myself. You've already done so much for me that I can't ask you to do this, too. Don't worry about me; I'll be fine. I bought a plane ticket last week, so I should be in Marfa by tomorrow morning. I'll come back once I've done it. I only hope you'll forgive me for not letting you come with me on this adventure.

I looked at the clock on the wall. If she had just left I could catch up to her at the airport. I ran for the front door and grabbed the keys to the truck. I made my way quickly down the stairs of our apartment and out into the parking lot where I could see the truck sitting.

On its side.

What the hell?

I got closer to inspect it and couldn't help but laugh. I punched the door and sat down on the ground staring at the front driver's side tire which she had let the air out before she left.

Jellyfish was bound and determined to do this without my help. All I could do was go back upstairs and wait for her to come back.

Twenty-One

2 Years Later - April 1980

I sighed as I made my way toward the abandoned railroad tracks. This was where I would come to clear my head. This is where I would come to throw rocks against the rusty train cars, and this is where I would come to tell myself that even though it had been two years, that Jellyfish was alive somewhere and would come back to me eventually.

Today, I pulled myself up into one of the cars and stretched out. I looked up through the rusty hole in the ceiling and wondered if she could see the same sky that I could see. I wondered if she loved the sky in Ontario as much as I did, and most of all, I wondered if she was in the sky watching me.

That was my biggest fear; that she had died alone. That she was dead at all. That I didn't get to tell her that I loved her one last time.

Snap out of it. You knew this would happen eventually.

I closed my eyes and took a deep breath of the crisp spring air and smiled. I shouldn't have been surprised that she had managed to outsmart me. Jellyfish was always one step ahead of me in every sense of the word. She was smaller, so she was faster. She was smarter, so she knew how to get what she wanted. She loved me, and she knew that I loved her, too, so I would do anything to make her happy.

I'll catch up to you one day, I thought with a chuckle. *You won't always be one step ahead of me.*

I didn't mean to, but I wound up taking a nap in the train car. I had been so damn tired lately, and I refused to get meds to sustain myself because if she couldn't use them, why should I? I still didn't show any signs of the marks she had but I was definitely becoming more aware of my sickness as the days passed.

But this was what I did with my days off. I would come out here and throw rocks and hang out, hoping that by the time I got home, she'd be there. Hoping that maybe I would bump into her on the street; something, *anything,* that would give me hope.

But so far, nothing.

That was until I decided to go home around one o'clock that afternoon and saw a large notice on the door stating that I had missed a delivery and that I would be able to go to the post office to pick it up.

I snatched the note off the door, shrugged, and walked back outside. The post office was only a mile away, and normally I would be able to walk that distance, but because of how tired I had been feeling lately, I had decided to drive.

I also managed to hit every red light on the way there. Needless to say, I was a bit moody when I walked in, but I went to the window and presented the notice and my identification. The window attendant disappeared with my information and about ten minutes later came back carrying a huge box, grunting from the effort of carrying it.

"Please sign here, Mr. Kenison," she said, sliding a form toward me. I read it briefly before I signed; it was just an acknowledgement of my receipt.

I picked up the box and walked out to the truck. I went around to the passenger's side and secured it with the seatbelt before I hopped back in the driver's seat and drove home. I drummed my fingers on the box in time with the song on the radio.

I got home a few moments later, miraculously hitting every green light this time, and grabbed the box and went back up the stairs into our apartment. I kicked the door closed behind me and set the box on the kitchen table. Then, I grabbed the toaster and threw a couple of pieces of bread in it. I went into the living room and turned the TV on so I could watch *Three's Company* while I waited for the toast to be ready.

I laughed as I watched the show and grabbed the butter from the refrigerator. The bread popped up, and I thinly layered butter onto it and watched the show a little longer before I went and sat at the table. Toast was the only thing these days that didn't make me ill.

I set my plate down and sighed when I saw all of the mailing tape all over the box and went over to the drawer in the kitchen to retrieve the largest, sharpest knife that we had.

Carefully, I sliced through the tape and opened the box. I pulled out an envelope and opened it up, but the burst of laughter from the TV audience got my attention. I set the letter down and watched the rest of the episode.

I didn't want to admit it to myself, but the worst feeling was growing over me the longer the box and the letter sat in front of me. I felt like I should be paying more attention to *it* than the television, so I walked into the living room and turned the TV off.

I finished my last piece of toast before I ripped the envelope open and read the contents. I let it fall from my hands, and I swallowed the hard lump in my throat. I flipped the lid of the cardboard box closed and inspected the return address.

Mr. and Mrs. Kenneth Parker. Marfa, TX.

I got shakily to my feet and looked into the box. There was another box of some kind inside. This one was made of some kind of ceramic. I pulled it out and set it on the table. My heart stopped beating for a moment; I swear it did. I fell back into my chair as I looked at the gold plate on the front of the box.

Betty Jo Parker
October 24, 1956 – January 1, 1980

I put my face on the table and I began to cry hysterically. In anger, in frustration, but most of all, in heartbreak. I knew what was in the heavy box that had come all the way from Marfa, Texas now. I knew that the girl I loved would never come home to me; not like I remembered her. Not smiling and mischievous, but as a pile of ashes with a message of hope and instructions to follow.

It's done.
Baker City, Marfa, Toledo, Durham, Baton-Rouge, New York City, Ontario.
The rest is yours.
Love always,
Jellyfish.

Grab your FREE copy of What Lies Beneath by scanning here:

"The atmosphere is dark and ominous, and there's seemingly no escape from the monster. But the question is, who is the real monster?"
-USA Today Bestselling Author Ellie Midwood

About The Author

Yolanda Olson is a USA Today Bestselling and award-winning author. Born and raised in Bridgeport, CT where she currently resides, she usually spends her time watching her favorite channel, Investigation Discovery. Occasionally, she takes a break to write books and test the limits of her mind. Also an avid horror movie fan, she like to incorporate dark elements into the majority of her books.

View Yolanda's books by scanning here: